Carol Smith, formerly a lead~~ing~~ ~~and~~ ~~...~~ now concentrates full-time on her writi~~ng career. She is the author~~ of the highly successful *Darkening Echoes*, *Kensington Court*, *Family Reunion*, *Unfinished Business*, *Grandmother's Footsteps*, *Hidden Agenda* and *Vanishing Point*. For more information about Carol Smith's books visit her website at *www.carolsmith.com*.

Praise for Carol Smith

Hidden Agenda
'Both a thriller – I was hooked by the very first page – and a gripping story about the power of female friendships – a winning combination!' Marika Cobbold

'A gripping and beautifully constructed story' Lizy Buchan

'Carol Smith has done it again, an unput-down-able thriller with a twist . . . Smith holds the reader in her grasp from start to finish, and gives us compelling psychological insights on the way' Julia Neuberger

Grandmother's Footsteps
'*Grandmother's Footsteps* . . . will keep you entertained, reading and guessing all the way to the end' *Crime Time*

'With its teasing insights into the mind of a serial killer, *Grandmother's Footsteps* keeps you guessing until the end' *Sainsbury's Magazine*

Unfinished Business
'If a pacy thriller is your thing, *Unfinished Business* will suit you to perfection . . . an addictive read' *Sunday Express*

'A thriller which certainly keeps you turning those pages . . . gripping right to the end' *Daily Mail*

Family Reunion
'A gripping read' *Family Circle*

'Full of action, twists and surprises, this intricate suspense story offers a fascinating new take on the nature of family ties' *Good Housekeeping*

Also by Carol Smith

DARKENING ECHOES
KENSINGTON COURT
DOUBLE EXPOSURE
FAMILY REUNION
UNFINISHED BUSINESS
GRANDMOTHER'S FOOTSTEPS
HOME FROM HOME
HIDDEN AGENDA
VANISHING POINT

CAROL SMITH

Without Warning

sphere

SPHERE

First published in Great Britain in 2006 by Time Warner Books
This paperback edition published in 2006 by Sphere

Copyright © Carol Smith 2006

The moral right of the author has been asserted.

A CIP catalogue record for this book
is available from the British Library.

ISBN-13: 978-0-751-53799-4
ISBN-10: 0-751-53799-3

Typeset in Berkeley Book by
Palimpsest Book Production Limited,
Grangemouth, Stirlingshire

Printed and bound in Great Britain by
Clays Ltd, St Ives plc

Sphere
An imprint of
Little, Brown Book Group
Brettenham House
Lancaster Place
London WC2E 7EN

A member of the Hachette Livre Group of Companies

www.littlebrown.co.uk

For Joanne Dickinson.
She knows why

Acknowledgements

Thanks, as always, to my wonderful publishers for doing their usual impeccable job. To Sarah Rustin and the rest of the team, especially Sales and Marketing. An additional thank you to Jenny Fry and Helen Gibbs for telling me stories about travelling by Tube which inspired me to write this book. And to Mark Thompson (formerly Metropolitan Police) for his helpful comments on police procedure. Also to my agents, Curtis Brown, for backing me up so well.

Prologue

The first time was almost an accident; an annoying woman, yapping into her phone, pushed in front of a train with the slightest of nudges. In the ensuing hullabaloo it wasn't hard to get lost in the crowd, though later he found the adrenalin fix lingered on. Killing was easy. It gave him a buzz and proved there were certain things that he *could* do.

The Tube was a relatively new experience which got him out of his virtual prison and enabled him to mix with the public at large. The incident had been spur of the moment, the victim chosen because of her manner and the way she ignored the commuters packed all around her. Though he was unable to catch what she was saying, the facial grimaces had been enough. She was overweight and her lipstick was smudged. He found her existence offensive. It took little more than a flick of the wrist to knock her off balance on her fashionable shoes and into the path of the approaching Circle Line train.

1

Alone and faceless in the milling crowd, he experienced a taste of what could be achieved. Next time he would come prepared and select his target more precisely.

Part One

Part One

1

The worst part was not being able to sleep, but he'd more or less given up on that since they'd started reducing the morphine that killed the pain. What he thought about most was the blinding flash and the disintegration of Finch's head when the booby trap he had failed to detect had blown up in their faces. In the months that followed he had tried to remember precisely what had led them to that spot. That particular spot, at that time, with its terrible denouement. For once his intelligence had proved faulty, the worst crime any surveillance expert could commit. Killing anyone was traumatic enough. To sacrifice a trusted partner was more than he could live with, even now.

Andy Brewster, ex-SAS, had returned from Baghdad a stretcher case, not entirely expected to walk again or even pull through. For months, as he'd lain in a hospital bed, slowly regaining the use of his legs, he'd gone endlessly over the nightmare scenario that would haunt him the rest of his life. He and

Finch had worked side by side for an unbroken seven years. The trust between them had been absolute though, naturally, never referred to. Yet Brewster had blundered and Finch had been killed; he knew the image would never be expunged. There were moments still when his courage almost failed and he longed to follow his partner into oblivion.

But Brewster was made of sterner stuff, despite the sweating and panic attacks; as his spine was fixed and his legs improved, so too did his fighting spirit. He knew he owed it to both of them to get back in the saddle as fast as he could to justify Finch's meaningless death by continuing with the fight. He had no inclination to do anything else, even if he'd had the choice. His fluent Arabic and knowledge of Islam had led him, via the Ministry of Defence, to this role as an undercover cop. Life on the edge really suited him best: he liked to stay constantly on his toes. His firearms training and specialist degree had led him to some of the world's hottest spots. He had kept super fit and emotionally free and worked out regularly in the gym. At forty-two he had been at his fighting best.

Not any more though. Since Iraq he'd had to learn to walk again. Now he could manage without his sticks, though occasionally used one to get around when the pain was at its most intense. He rapidly weaned himself off the drugs, having seen how pernicious such a habit could become; was determined not to give in to terrorists. He had begged to be allowed to return to work, to leave the confines of the hospital, which was rapidly driving him out of his mind with a suffocating ennui. Also to help him repay the debt, to give back something in recompense for having been the unwitting cause of the wasteful death of his friend.

*   *   *

After much deliberation and the usual red tape, they'd seconded him to the Metropolitan Police, working plainclothes on the transit system, using his espionage expertise in the fight against terrorist crime. It was not a job he particularly relished yet it fell within his limited scope until he had fully regained his strength and been given a clean bill of health. At this time of year, at the height of the season, with the tourist invasion beginning to peak, anti-terrorist skills like his were at their most essential. And it certainly beat a desk-bound job, a death-knell to the active career he fervently hoped he would some day be able to resume.

His initial reaction to Burgess, his new partner, had been cautious in the extreme. After what he'd seen happen to Finch, he'd have far preferred to have worked on his own, for the symbiosis between partners is crucial and he wasn't yet ready to bond again. But police regulations said he must have one and Burgess possessed credentials he couldn't replicate. At first they'd regarded each other with caution, then taken a walk to break the ice, and Brewster, rather to his surprise, had found himself quickly won over. Despite the fact he was trained to kill, Burgess had such an equable nature that it only took a matter of days for them to become trusted pals.

They had settled down to a steady routine that varied little from day to day. Brewster hated the Underground, missed the exotic delights of Baghdad, but his new companion made it easier to adjust. Furthermore, there was no denying that Burgess certainly knew his stuff. Like it or not, they were stuck with each other, certainly till the end of the season. The job was tedious but had to be done. One blink and a deadly device could go off or something nasty be hidden beneath a seat. And at least it beat mouldering away in retirement like so many of his former colleagues. He enjoyed being part of the ebb and flow of the city's daily life.

What he hadn't expected though, quite so soon, was to witness first hand the terrible damage a train can do to a person beneath its wheels.

At first it had looked like an accident: the victim had stumbled and lost her balance as the rush hour crowd surged forward, out of control. It had meant total closure of the Circle Line for the minimum two and a half hours it took for the police and emergency services to come through. They had raised her carefully from the track and placed her remains in a body bag. It was only when they turned her over that what had happened became apparent. Deliberately killed in the rush hour crowds, yet no one appeared to have seen a thing. At least, no witnesses had so far come forward.

The few they'd questioned had noticed nothing. All they recalled was the usual swirl of people pressing forward as the train approached and then the blood-curdling scream. It had taken the transport police an age to curb the panic and calm them all down. It wasn't a bomb or a terror attack, just a horrible, meaningless tragedy caused by too many people on the platform at one time.

'I blame the council,' an official declared. 'If it weren't for this damned congestion charge people would still be using their cars and these incidents wouldn't occur.'

But then, of course, they'd discovered the knife and the Metropolitan Police were drafted in.

2

It was ten to nine and the platform was packed. The Underground system was still snarled up by Friday's horrible murder. All the papers had carried the story though none appeared to have any real lead. A bank cashier, who had worked in Moorgate, had fallen beneath an Underground train while talking on her mobile to a friend. It now turned out that she had been stabbed, incredible with so many people about. Beth loathed the Tube, especially in rush hour, but at this time of day it was the preferable option. The traffic along the Bayswater Road would be at its usual standstill. Duncan kept urging her to take a cab but she knew, from grim experience, how hard that could be. Compared to hers, his journey was simple: two stops anti-clockwise to Gloucester Road. If he felt in the mood, he could easily walk, as occasionally in the summer he did. He liked the stroll over Kensington Church Street, with its rows of classy antiques shops.

Beth shoved her way along the platform to be closer to the Baker Street exit, and surged with the crowd when the train came in, disgorging a sprinkling of tourists. She wriggled her way to a corner by the doors, trying to avoid too much bodily contact. The journey was only five stops but absolute hell. She was used to it now, had been doing it for years since she took the decision to give up her catering career. Running a shop was hard enough but not nearly as stressful as wedding receptions or boardroom lunches for stuffy men in suits.

The woman standing opposite was familiar: Beth had noticed her many times before. She also travelled to Baker Street every morning. They would climb the steps to the street side by side but not, by so much as a glance, acknowledge each other. Typical of the Brits, she thought; in almost any other city in the world they'd be swapping jokes and on first-name terms by now. Except for New York, where they'd be cursing each other in a frantic jostle to reach the turnstile first. Beth grinned; one day she'd surprise them both and venture a tentative 'Good morning'.

Celeste was also aware of Beth, a pretty woman who was often privately smiling. She envied her; from the wedding ring it would seem that she wasn't alone in the world. She looked like someone at peace with herself who paid little heed to the laughter lines, her thickening waist or the first faint touches of grey. Not so Celeste, who hated herself as much as she hated life in general, had done so since the catastrophe that had stopped her career before it had even begun.

She had once lived the life of a pampered princess, spoilt and indulged by adoring parents who had given her every advantage in life, including an opulent home. No expense had ever been spared; she had ballet classes and deportment lessons and her clothes, like her mother's, were couture made in Paris. Her future, it had been assumed, was already completely mapped out. With looks like hers, plus the family name, she was destined surely to shoot to the top. Stardom was hers for the taking, once she was ready. She had grown up haughty and condescending, aware of the admiring looks but too aloof to acknowledge her would-be suitors.

Until the terrible thing occurred, after which her life had drastically altered. Instead of becoming a movie star, she'd been forced to quit RADA in her second year and now was stuck in this tedious job that she felt was unworthy of her talents. It wasn't fair; it had not been her fault that the sole inheritance they'd left was the house, these days shabby after years of neglect, plus the problem it contained. For, no matter how much she disliked her work, going home at night was the hardest part, having to deal with a situation from which she could never escape.

Consulting hours were 9.30 to 5. She must get a move on or else she'd be late. It was seven minutes to Devonshire Place then another five down to Wimpole Street. With luck, she'd be there before His Nibs and have the coffee on by the time he arrived.

They were late that morning leaving the flat, because they'd stayed up too late the night before and Alice had said they must first make things shipshape for the cleaner.

'You are *so* middle class,' scoffed Julie from Bradford, running her fingers through her spiked-up hair and checking her iPod was properly charged for the journey. In her ultra-short skirt and cork-heeled wedges, she was the epitome of groovy chic. She worked in women's features for the *Daily Mail*. Alice's male friends found her slightly alarming.

'Then go on without me,' Alice said calmly, rinsing glasses and stacking plates. She had been taught, from an early age, always to clear up after herself and not leave a mess for the cleaner to have to deal with.

Which was something Julie could not comprehend. 'Why keep a dog and bark yourself?' she said.

Alice smiled. It was hard to explain but, nevertheless, she dried her hands, removed her apron and relented. They were lucky to have a cleaner at all but that was what sharing a flat entailed. For a small extra cost, it gave them domestic freedom. Onslow Gardens was close to the Tube; they would be there in just a few minutes. They discussed what to do about supper that night, then went their separate ways.

The *Daily Mail* was only two stops away. If it weren't for the height of her heels she could almost have walked it. It was a stroke of luck having Alice to share with; though earning quite well for her twenty-two years, Julie was an inveterate shopaholic. And Kensington High Street was packed with clothes; it was only lucky that her hours were so long. If she didn't love the job so much, she might well have packed it in.

She had served her apprenticeship on a Bradford paper then moved to London as soon as she could. Had been living in the YWCA when, fortuitously, she'd met Alice on a typing course and the two of them had become friends. Alice was posh, in a low-key way, and worked in a bookshop, which was badly paid but the only thing she had ever really wanted to do. When her flatmate got married, she'd invited Julie to move in. They were chalk and cheese but got along well, mainly since Alice was so easy-going and Julie put a bit of zip into her life.

Julie herself was fiercely ambitious and longing to have her own by-line. She was good at the job and a very hard worker though inclined to be confrontational which put up her colleagues' backs. Apart from Alice, her friends were mostly male. She hung around the bars with them after work.

Wilbur and Ellie got on at Tower Hill, having started their sightseeing early. With only five days before moving on, Wilbur was keen to fit everything in, though secretly Ellie preferred a more leisurely pace. She would have preferred to have seen some street life, not just the tourist sights. That was her husband all over, however; he was not yet used to not having a business to run. It was just one stop to Monument, after which, she had a nasty suspicion, he was going to expect her to tramp around all day.

He had studied the map over early breakfast and made a list of the things he wanted to see. St Paul's Cathedral came top of his list and then, surprisingly, the Bank of England, whereas Ellie would have liked to browse in Spitalfields market or cross the river to the new Tate Modern and take in some art after having a leisurely lunch. But Wilbur, at seventy, had in no way eased off. She wasn't sure she'd survive another four days.

Her married life had not been eventful: two daughters, now grown, were all she felt she'd achieved. Chippewa Falls was pleasant enough and she'd made good friends there over the years, but Wilbur's retirement had meant a considerable change. In place of a quiet domestic life, baking and cleaning and bottling preserves, she now had him home all day, getting under her feet. Golf still occupied much of his time and that was a heaven-sent blessing, but his presence interfered with her charity work and the coffee mornings she ran for the church and meant she had a lot less time for herself and her cultural activities. Along with being his general factotum, she was now his social secretary as well.

'We're here,' he announced. They had reached their stop. Ellie obediently fell into step behind him.

Margaret changed trains at Victoria station, heading for Kensington High Street. She was making a tapestry cushion for the den and needed to buy more wools from Ehrmanns, the only place she knew of that still supplied them. She loathed the crowds, wasn't used to them, but at least today the Circle Line wasn't too packed. A smiling busker came through the carriage, playing guitar rather well. She gave him a pound. After Haywards Heath, it was quite a culture shock. She came into London so rarely these days, for urgent shopping or to see an exhibition. Since Jack had died she had been on her own. The boys were both busy with their careers and neither daughter-in-law seemed to care for her much.

After she'd done her bit of shopping, she'd walk through the park to the V&A or else get back on the Tube for the two-station ride. She must start heading home by mid-afternoon, before the early rush hour got under way. The train was usually packed after that and she wanted to be sure of a seat. There'd been a nasty incident the previous week that had hit all the front pages. A woman had fallen in front of a train; it was even suggested she might have been pushed. Margaret shuddered. At times life was very unpleasant. She missed not having her husband around, hated entering the empty house knowing there wouldn't be anyone there to greet her. She took out her book; it was only four stops but she couldn't wait to finish the last few chapters.

3

Imogen enjoyed a long lie-in, something she did a lot these days. She was rarely home before half past one and her mother said she could do with the extra rest. She rose at eleven, had a leisurely soak, then called her friend Alice on her mobile phone.

'Hi,' she said, biting into a peach and stretching out on the sofa to chat. She was part of the chorus of *Anything Goes* and wasn't required at the theatre till a quarter past six.

'Can't talk now,' said Alice, sounding rushed. She ran the bookshop almost single-handed with only part-time help.

'So call me back,' said Imogen benignly. The problem with working nights was the empty days.

She scrambled eggs in her mother's pristine kitchen, trying hard not to make a mess. Since Beth had given up catering, they mainly ate out. Then she settled down to watch *Cash in the Attic*, keenly observed by two hopeful dogs, slavering for a snack.

'Come here, you.' She tugged one over, dropping a kiss on its satin-smooth snout. The dogs belonged to her stepfather, Duncan, and often went with him to work. She loved the setup now; her mother had never seemed happier.

Beth, in the shop, was working flat out, serving a queue of early lunchers who came in droves every day at this time in search of her famous homemade snacks. Though primarily a delicatessen, the shop also had an area at the back which laid on a grazing menu for famished shoppers. The work was hard but preferable to cooking. At least she now had her evenings and weekends free.

She took a breather to call her husband, to check how his day was going.

'Good,' he said. They had saved a Burmese cat's life.

'That's wonderful, darling.' He was a brilliant vet, as immersed in his career as she was in hers. The pivotal point of her life had been when they'd met.

'I have to get back.' They both worked hard but liked to make contact whenever they could. Imogen laughed and called them soppy, but only ever with a twinkle in her eye. Life had improved for her as well when they'd finally got it together.

They arranged to eat at home that night and Beth made a note to take something back. There was a movie on he wanted to see which suited her fine as well. With Imogen out six nights a week, their cosy twosome had been restored. She missed her daughter and worried about her but also enjoyed being back in honeymoon mode. It made her feel young and frisky again. She hoped she'd get home in time to wash her hair.

'Bye, darling,' she said. 'See you at seven.'

'Can't wait. I'll try not to be late.'

*　　*　　*

Their first appointment was a teenage girl with a nose too large for her delicate face. She'd been brought by an overbearing mother who did all the talking and made one thing clear: she wanted her daughter fixed for her social debut. The doctor tactfully said very little but carefully scrutinised the patient before taking preliminary Polaroids for his own use. He smiled at her, which helped her relax, and made her lie back on the comfortable couch while he flashed a series of slides on the screen before her.

'It is your choice,' he said. 'There are several that would suit you. You'll be beautiful, I promise, when I am done.'

The girl, overwhelmed with embarrassment, carefully studied each picture. Then turned her head to look at Celeste, still hovering in the doorway. 'I'd like to look like her,' she whispered and the mother nodded her approval.

'What do you think, Celeste?' asked the doctor, accustomed to patients reacting this way. 'That's why I keep her around,' he explained, with a wink. 'She's a great advertisement for my work.' A tired old joke; Celeste merely smiled and went back to her case notes. The only part of the job she could bear was witnessing the happiness surgery could bring. With a smaller nose that child would be transformed, might even end up pretty. The mother was right; the ugly duckling deserved the chance to become a swan. The details were discussed and a date was set. They could fit her in at the start of next year which would mean she'd be fully recovered in time for her ball. Celeste gave the mother a list of dos and don'ts – no alcohol, avoid these foods – and promised to phone a few days in advance to remind them of the appointment.

'Don't worry,' she said as she saw them out. 'Dr Rousseau is world famous. Without doubt, the best plastic surgeon we have in this country.'

'Well, if you are anything to go by,' said the mother. The daughter was far too timid to speak at all.

Celeste gave her enigmatic smile and stood at the top of the stairs to watch them leave. They shared the elegant house with three other surgeons.

The next one in was a much older woman with the tight strained look of a habitual addict; she was far too thin, with a startled Bambi look. When she filled in the forms, Celeste was proved right. A surgery junkie, destroying herself. She really believed that no one out there would ever notice. Celeste showed her in to talk to the doctor, then closed the door and returned to her notes. He would set her right, being deeply committed to making his patients look better not worse. Which, in this case, would require considerable tact. She made more coffee – it was almost eleven – then studied herself in the glass. If only her life had turned out as intended, she wouldn't be here, in this menial job, paying lip service to spoilt rich women and emotional cripples.

Two perfect murders had made him restless. The buzz in his head stopped him sleeping. He got up early and went downstairs. While the kettle boiled, he opened a drawer and stared at the rows of gleaming knives, carefully stored in their green baize slots, untouched for so many years. He tested the blades with a practised finger and found them as sharp as they had been then, a sensation that made him shiver and feel slightly giddy. He closed his eyes and his senses whirled, stirred by the memory of what they could do. The moment of impact, the scream, the blood; the release he felt when the blade went in, as smoothly as slicing through butter. He had watched her fall and the blood gush forth in a foaming arc that had soaked his hair. He closed his eyes in an effort to block it out.

He had started to sweat at the recollection, so made his coffee and took two pills to try to calm himself down. He had felt the moment it punctured her lung, the hysteria of the crowd as she toppled forward. Had watched the train as it neatly sliced her in two. There'd been panic then and such pandemonium that he'd had no reason to hurry away. He had hung around to see what happened next. Since childhood that was what he had been: a silent observer on the sidelines of life. A watcher whom no one had ever even noticed.

But now he had a new incentive. It was growing late and time to go. He picked up his bag, slipped his sunglasses on and let himself out of the house.

By the end of the day, as they headed home, Ellie found herself distinctly flagging. Though twelve years older, Wilbur took the pace in his stride, seemed scarcely out of breath. By Victoria station the train was packed, the evening rush hour well under way, and a nice young man with excellent manners stood up and offered his seat. For a moment Ellie thought it was Wilbur who should sit but she knew his pride wouldn't countenance that. Wisconsin males went out of their way to take proper care of their ladies. It would almost have been a duelling point should the young man have offered it to him.

'All right, dear?' He smiled down at her, his broad face flushed in the stifling heat. He removed his plaid jacket and loosened his tie. She could see he was heavily perspiring.

'Here, give me that.' She held out her hand and took the jacket, leaving Wilbur free and unencumbered, studying the map.

'Tomorrow,' he told her, 'we will go upriver to look at

Greenwich and Canary Wharf. I am sure you would like a nice ride on a boat. And afterwards we'll go to Hampton Court.'

She nodded and smiled. At least on a boat she'd be sitting down and she liked the prospect of seeing a royal palace. But it wasn't enough. It was her trip too, and inside Ellie was seething. Europe had always been one of her dreams, something they'd never been able to do. The kids were too small or they hadn't the money or Wilbur was too busy with his golf. They were finally here but nothing had changed. Wilbur was making all the decisions, barely aware that his wife might have preferences too. Tonight they had tickets for *The Lion King*; he had heard that the show was not to be missed and he'd booked the Strand Palace for a meal afterwards.

Though unimaginative, Wilbur meant well. It was not his fault that their tastes were so different, though it might have helped if he ever stopped to listen to what she had to say. He treated her, as he always had, as the child bride he had snatched from her studies, without ever stopping to think that she still had a brain. But the train was already at Gloucester Road. She rose and followed him once again for the arduous evening slog down the Cromwell Road.

4

In those long arid months while he'd lain in bed, encased in plaster, unable to move, Brewster's awareness had been a living nightmare. Over and over he had replayed the shattering explosion of the booby trap, the moment when the bomb had gone off, blowing their jeep to pieces. How he'd survived was a mystery; he had dragged himself from the wreckage with oil in his hair and blood all over his face and clothes. Finch's blood. Those of the team who had also escaped had covered him as he crawled away and later an army helicopter had airlifted him to safety. The rest of that period remained a blur. He only knew how lucky he was to be alive.

Later, after they'd moved him to Bournemouth and a nurse started pushing him out for walks, the sting of the salt in the air had begun to revive him. The skirl of the gulls had a soothing effect so that, after a while, he could sleep again. Nature was aiding the long slow haul to recovery. Though the terrible image of what had occurred was etched indelibly into his brain. From that point on, he was emotionally barren.

It was during that time, as he practised walking, that Brewster had taken up painting. As a boy he had been an accomplished draughtsman, though in the tough circles he moved in then such skills had been dismissed as being sissy. He'd forgotten about it for several decades until an elderly aunt came to visit, bringing a child's set of crayons and a sketchpad.

'Something to help you fill in the hours.' She remembered the Christmas cards he had drawn as a child.

Brewster, startled, had muttered his thanks then shoved the package to the back of a drawer. These days he couldn't even read, he was so despondent. But then, as he idled, with time on his hands, and the bright clear light from the sea had inspired him, he delved back into the drawer and rescued the pad.

At first he started with simple things: a chair, a jug, an arrangement of flowers, even a sketch of the chambermaid when she came in to change the sheets. Later he sent out for charcoal and paper, the thick matt kind he remembered from school. And a slim tin box of watercolour paints and a bunch of sable brushes. The nursing staff were pleased with his progress; his constitution improved along with his art. Also, to his surprise, his spirits. The future no longer seemed quite as grim. He was slowly beginning to live again, not before it was time.

'Are you planning to sell them?' another patient asked.

'You have to be out of your mind,' he growled. But, nevertheless, the remark raised his spirits and made him that much more determined. Painting helped him focus his mind and expel the nightmares. In his darker moments, since he'd been discharged, his mood swings were mirrored in what he produced. It slowly began to dawn on him what a great catharsis art was.

Since he'd moved to the Metropolitan Police he hadn't had time to start painting again. Till now he had not felt the need.

Once the morning rush hour had slackened off, Brewster and Burgess came into their own, working methodically through the train, permanently on the alert. They acted as if they were ordinary passengers and kept a very low profile. Occasionally they would alter their pace and sit for a while to rest Brewster's leg and keep an eye on what was happening around them. They concentrated on the comings and goings, who got on and off at each stop. Brewster's memory was photographic; once he registered a face, he rarely forgot it. Commuters had their own regular patterns, depending on their destinations. In a couple of weeks he started to recognise people.

They began at Cannon Street, where they were based, and did the whole circuit clockwise. At the City stations it was bankers in suits, frenetically gabbling into their phones as they scurried off, always late no matter how early. Temple was barristers carrying wig-bags; Embankment the bulk of the tourist trade. The river boats and the London Eye as well as the bridge to the Festival Hall. They travelled in herds and, when they got off, the air felt that much fresher. Westminster was Parliament, which meant more tourists, including the ones en route to the Abbey. St James's Park was the passport office, where students and all sorts of backpackers swarmed, then Victoria – one of the main-line stations – where the carriages filled up again. Sloane Square was shoppers and ladies in hats, with their braying voices and silly laughs. Brewster winced; more than anyone else, he loathed well-bred women like that. It took him back to his early days as a hoodlum from the north.

At Gloucester Road a busker got on, methodically working his way through the train, expertly playing guitar Bruce Springsteen-style. He glanced at the cops, who gave nothing away. Brewster stopped himself just in time from flicking a coin in his cap. These days buskers were becoming a menace, Romanian gypsies the worst of the lot. Kids as young as eight or less with instruments they couldn't play. In his uniform days he would caution them but they took little notice. Begging, for them, was a way of life; he had learned to turn a blind eye. This guy, however, was the real McCoy, with a soaring talent that startled Brewster and took him back to the days of his youth when he'd played in a student band. This guy had a story he'd like to hear; he was sorry to see him move on.

At the end of the carriage sat a grave young man, impeccably dressed in a business suit, apparently reading the *Financial Times* but never once turning the pages. Brewster watched him and wondered where he was heading at this time of day. He looked a typical City type yet had stayed on through all the obvious stations. It seemed an odd time to be going home. At least he didn't have a backpack.

South Kensington was museum traffic; masses more shoppers at High Street Ken. By now both partners were feeling peckish so they'd take a break at Notting Hill Gate. This was already their second time round this morning.

It was sobering to think that, among all these masses, someone was out there playing dangerous games with a knife.

When he saw the damage the train had done, Brewster had almost thrown up. Death was one thing, but mutilation . . . the mental image of Finch exploding triggered the images in his head and brought the nightmares back. Yet by the time she fell under the wheels, the bank cashier was almost certainly dead.

24

Someone had knifed her so hard in the back, it had pushed her under the train. The killer had taken a terrible risk of being caught on closed-circuit TV but, as it was, the cameras had failed to record it. All that showed up on the grainy footage was a moving mass of people packed tight and the sudden confusion as the train pulled in.

Brewster wondered who would take such a risk when a back-street stabbing would have done the job. Surely only a certified madman would chance it. They had brought in the people closest to her, her boyfriend and colleagues at the bank, then let them go because they had alibis. Kimberley Martin was just a statistic. He filed the interviews away.

5

Dancing was in Imogen's blood. Both her parents had been on the stage; it was how they had first met. Beth had not wanted her to turn professional, had herself given it up at roughly that age and taken the far more sensible step of learning to cook for a living. But in matters like that her ex, Gus Hardy, invariably prevailed. His daughter, he said, was born to dance, with her mother's height and his own agility. Although, these days, he stayed mainly on the coast, he kept in touch and watched Imogen's progress with pride. From a gawky child she had grown into a woman, slimmer than Beth and more finely boned, with glossy dark hair and those great trusting eyes that came from her father's genes. Gus was right to be proud of his daughter; they both were. And the marital split seemed not to have damaged her at all.

She got on brilliantly with Duncan too, a secret relief to Beth. His knack with animals included kids; he had guided Imogen through her teen years as if she were his own. Beth's sole regret, which she kept to herself, was that she'd not managed a baby with him. Her childbearing years had been almost over by the time they had first got together. Imogen, though, was an absolute joy. Beth loved it that Imogen still lived at home, dreaded the time, which could not be far off, when she finally spread her wings and flew the nest.

The journey to the National Theatre could not have been more straightforward. Imogen took the Tube to Embankment then walked across Hungerford Bridge. The sun was brilliant, though starting to sink as she elbowed her way through the rush hour crowds. Her mobile rang; Alice at last, finally returning her call.

'I'm on the train,' said Alice primly, at which they both shrieked with mirth. The silly cliché had become their code. Thank God for friends who were on your wavelength. No need to mention the quaking nerves; they had been together since infanthood. Alice always understood these things.

Imogen gradually slackened her pace, her phone still pressed to her ear. Every few yards along the river live acts performed for the strolling crowds, part of the free street theatre of the South Bank. There were acrobats and performance artists, doing all manner of dangerous things. If it weren't for the fact she was due on stage, she'd be strongly tempted to hang around. She loved the ambience of the place, especially in summer.

Posed on a box beneath the trees a living statue was doing his thing, bronzed all over and eerily still, even his eyeballs unmoving. Unlike the angel and the painted clown, this one wore very male attire, with boots and breeches and gauntleted gloves like an old-fashioned aviator. Imogen paused to look at him, finding the blank eyes disconcerting. He could have been genuinely made out of bronze, showed no sign even of breathing. She looked at him and he looked back. Something about that unwavering stare unnerved her. There were mimes in most of the tourist spots; she saw them whenever she travelled abroad. Clever, maybe, and often inventive, but still decidedly creepy.

'I'd best get on,' she said to Alice, having lost her desire for an intimate chat. 'The curtain goes up in less than an hour and I've still got my make-up to do.'

They made a date for later that week; then Imogen, still experiencing a thrill, proudly walked through the doors of the National Theatre.

Margaret retraced her tracks to Victoria, keen now to catch her train and be gone. She had bought her wools and another canvas that should keep her occupied into the winter or, at the very least, for another few months. The Arts and Crafts exhibition had been lovely, providing inspiration for things she might do. Room by room, she was sprucing up the house; it kept her busy and stopped the endless brooding. She'd converted Jack's den into her sewing room and often went up there in the afternoon for a long luxurious read. Her love of books had proved a great solace and helped fill in the empty hours. She glanced round at her fellow travellers. Whereas once they would have been reading papers, now it was paperback books. Due, no doubt, to the cramped conditions but excellent for the book trade.

It was also hot; she dabbed at her neck, relieved to be leaving town. A few hours in this stifling city was as much as she could endure these days, though she also found herself energised by the crowds. She had always been the active one, while Jack had preferred to potter at home. It was quite an event when she got him to come into London. The familiar misery rose in her throat. His death had been dreadfully sudden. Just as they'd faced their golden years he was gone.

A blind man and his dog got on; she contemplated giving up her seat but a young man in a dark City suit beat her to it. She watched as the blind man carefully settled, wondering how he could manage on his own. There were all kinds of loneliness in the world, something she'd never thought of. He was rather striking, tall and well built with an interesting face and sensitive mouth. He wore black glasses with opaque lenses; the dog was an Alsatian. She stooped to pat it and it licked her hand. Jack would have liked a dog but had been asthmatic.

Alice and Julie met for a pizza at the Pheasantry, where they could sit outside. It was almost July and the days were long though by this time pleasantly cooler. Julie was late, which was nothing new, held up, she said, by an editorial crisis. She enjoyed her job, as Alice did hers, had her sights fixed firmly on one day having her own column. She was wearing one of her very short skirts with wedge-heeled sandals that tied with bows. Her hair was artfully waxed into spikes which gave her the look of a cockatoo. She was pretty, in a rather offbeat way, though inclined to spoil the effect by being too abrasive. Alice admired her sardonic wit but knew that others found her hard to take. She drank too much and was then inclined to get vicious.

Imogen at first hadn't warmed to her at all, jealous, perhaps, of the two girls' closeness since Alice had always been her own best friend. Lately, however, she was coming round and starting to find her tremendous fun. Julie was fearless and often outrageous whereas Alice, even at the best of times, could be prim.

'Hiya!' said Julie, flopping down and instantly lighting up, another habit that Alice's friends couldn't stand. Alice ordered a tuna salad, Julie her favourite American Hot. With a bottle of house red and two glasses of water.

'How are things?' Julie wanted to know and Alice filled her in on the state of the book trade. Sales were poor and increasingly sluggish; the supermarkets threatened to close the independents down. She might even end up losing her job but books were where her heart had always been set. One day she was hoping to write herself but was far too modest ever to let Julie know that.

Julie asked how Imogen was and Alice said they had spoken an hour ago. 'She works terribly hard,' she said with pride. 'Eight performances every week, plus daily rehearsals and having to keep herself fit.'

'But she doesn't work in the mornings,' said Julie, who would herself have occasionally liked to sleep in. She was a party girl who stayed out late and drank far more than was good for her. And the writing part of the job could be very exacting. She made it look easy by knocking things off but rarely mentioned the research that lay behind it.

She was slightly in awe of Alice's friend, with her supple body and stunning looks and the type of skin that is just as good without make-up. Since Imogen was dancing almost every night, Julie had not really got to know her. But she liked what she saw and envied Imogen's talent. She had seen the show a couple of times and hoped to do so again, but felt awkward even suggesting it in case Alice felt she was pushy.

Alice, however, could read her thoughts and was touched by Julie's sensitivity. 'I'm seeing her later this week,' she said. 'If you'd care to tag along.'

They finished their meal and then drifted home through the lustrous foliage of Chelsea. They would probably watch a DVD and open another bottle of wine. It was great to be single and independent in the summer of 2005.

It was almost eight when Celeste got home, having taken a detour through Selfridges, not that she needed any new clothes or, indeed, had anywhere to wear them. The house was silent as she opened the door; all she could hear was the grandfather clock and the distant thrum of the fridge motor ticking over. The air was stale, the windows all shut, and the scent of decay and yesterday's lamb hung heavily in the air. She carried her packages through to the kitchen and switched on the kettle for a cup of tea. There was vodka chilling in the freezer drawer but the later she started on that, the better. She would eat her palm hearts and beetroot salad and check what was on TV.

He was out as usual; his door was closed but she knew he wasn't there from the absolute stillness. Over the years she'd become adept at picking up on the slightest sound. Even his breathing at times could drive her crazy. She'd been blessed with looks that might have made her fortune but instead served only as a magnet to fools who believed that happiness lay in superficial perfection. If they knew what she did, they'd think twice before wasting their money.

She changed out of her working clothes and into her ancient

32

kaftan. There was nothing but *Big Brother* to watch and that she could easily do without. With a sigh, she collected the bottle from the freezer and took it upstairs for an early night. With luck, she wouldn't even hear him when he came home.

6

The boat was breezy but Ellie kept quiet. It was better than having to walk all day and she found its gliding progress oddly soothing. It was fully packed, with every seat taken, so she dared not leave hers for even a second for fear of having it snatched. Wilbur, as usual, was striding around, taking endless photos that no one would look at but might prove a conversational topic back home. She watched him as he stood at the prow, the breeze from the water ruffling his hair, a fine-looking man though sixty pounds overweight. His military bearing belied his true status, glued to a desk for most of his life, running the business inherited from his forebears. Nothing glamorous about fertiliser except that it had kept them in style for most of the thirty-eight years they had been married. He had always thrown his weight about, the more so now he was retired. His booming baritone competed with the commentary that she, for one, was straining to hear. Had he been nearer she'd have asked him to shush but, for once, he was keeping his distance, enabling her to pretend she was travelling alone.

The couple beside her had brought their lunch. 'Bit breezy today,' said the woman.

'Indeed,' said Ellie, producing a scarf and wrapping it tightly round her ears to keep them from dropping off. The boat was heading for Canary Wharf and then on to Greenwich where the *Cutty Sark* was moored. After that they would catch the next one back, all the way down to Hampton Court for Ellie to get a glimpse of the palace, though they'd have to move pretty sharpish. Another day without proper sustenance; she wished she had also thought of bringing a picnic. The man went down to the bar for drinks and offered to bring Ellie something back. They thought she was on her own. Would that she was.

'Thanks, but no,' she said with a smile. 'My husband will fetch me something later.' He was leaning comfortably on the rail, chatting away to a couple of men, clearly throwing his weight around, oblivious of her needs. With an audience he'd be happy for hours. She decided to move inside, away from the breeze. She pointed him out to the friendly woman and asked her to kindly let him know where she'd gone. She might have told him herself but couldn't be bothered.

'Men,' said the woman, with a complicit smile.

'Indeed,' said Ellie as she left.

The downstairs lounge was hazy with smoke but at least she was out of the wind. And now could easily hear the commentary. She settled in a corner and loosened her scarf; what she'd really like was a cup of tea but the fifty storeys of Canary Wharf were fast bearing down upon them. Time to move; Wilbur was beckoning, having finally noticed her absence. No peace for the wicked. She rose to her feet and wearily went to join him.

Julie, for once, was in on time since she had a very tight copy date and prided herself on always meeting deadlines. As she rode the long escalator up to her floor, her mind was buzzing with feature ideas. Her copy was due in at noon and she still hadn't thought of an angle. Cautious Alice, who was conscientious, admired this devil-may-care attitude; one of the reasons she so much liked sharing with Julie.

'I'd never have the courage,' she said, 'having always been such a tedious swot. At school I did my weekend homework on Fridays.'

'That's what it's all about,' explained Julie. 'Living on the edge.' She needed the last-minute panic to make it work. It was one of the reasons she was so good, the constant ability to think on her feet. She relied on her fertile and active brain to get her through any crisis. It was ten by the time she had sorted her mail. Two hours till deadline; well, she'd been in tighter spots. She walked to the window and gazed out at the church, desperately seeking inspiration.

'If you've nothing better to do with your time,' said Rupert Lascelles, the theatre critic, 'you might care to help me out with a spot of research.'

Julie gave him her slant-eyed look. She wasn't a bloody researcher. Nor, for that matter, was she part of his team.

'Don't worry,' said Rupert, who knew her well. 'I'll see that you get a proper credit.' Money, too; there'd be cash in hand. Julie, he knew from experience, drove a hard bargain. He dumped a pile of buff folders on her desk. 'It's part of a series I'm working on for Hallmark. With luck, there will also be a tie-in book.'

Julie liked Rupert, who was caustic but brilliant and whose savage one-liners made her laugh. 'Deal,' she said, 'on one condition. Give me a subject for a fast four-hundred-word filler.'

'Ladies' fashions at Wimbledon this week? What the Williams sisters are wearing. Or else the Live8 concert in Hyde Park. There has to be some sort of hidden agenda. Those guys can't be that altruistic.'

'Wicked!' said Julie. How naff could one be, but celebrity pieces never failed. And Venus was tipped to win the championship again. Four hundred words on how cool she was would beautifully fill the slot.

The shop stayed open till half past nine, though Beth only rarely stayed there that late, an advantage of being the boss, she was fond of saying. Her team was efficient and able to cope. There were far fewer people around at that hour, mainly locals buying their supper or office workers in search of something to eat. The grazing room did a fairly brisk trade which also boosted regular sales as customers often then bought food to take home. The shop specialised in cheeses and charcuterie, own-baked breads and patisserie as well as superior wines and homemade truffles.

Tonight, however, would be an exception. Beth had stayed late in order to audit the books. At this time of year, when the pressure was off, she always did an in-depth stocktaking, making lists of things to cancel or replace. She liked this chore, even though it took hours, since it gave her a sense of how well they were doing. She had built the business from scratch and was making it work. On nights like this, when she got home really late, the last thing she wanted was to have to cook, so they almost always ate out.

It was hot when she finally wound down the shutters and the street still thronged with people. Summer in London in weather like this was almost like being in Paris or Rome. There were café tables out on the pavements and packs of young people round the pubs. She stopped to buy some cut-price flowers for the house.

She considered waiting for the 27 bus, then decided it would take too long. She needed to get home by the fastest route. They would drink outside on the patio tonight and book a table for after ten. As she wandered towards Baker Street, she dreamily savoured what she would eat, the special pasta at Assaggi or seafood at Kensington Place. Life with Duncan was a lasting delight because they had so many tastes in common. And never ever were short of things to discuss.

There were people milling around at the station, more than usual at this time of night. Beth heaved an utterly weary sigh; the last thing she needed when she was so tired was another bloody hold-up. She reached the turnstiles, travel card ready, but before she got there she saw the board. Long delays due to an incident, it read. The service was suspended.

Another horrible death, it turned out, only five days after the last one.

7

This time the murder was not at rush hour but at 8.47, when things were much quieter, before the theatre and restaurant crowds came out. Another young woman, again stabbed to death. She'd been standing alone on Baker Street station, presumably waiting for a Circle Line train; pretty and stylish, perhaps in her thirties, chatting cheerfully on her phone, just like the previous victim, Kimberley Martin. Several passengers claimed to have seen her, though none had been witness to the actual attack which must have occurred straight after the train she hadn't got on had pulled out. Brewster and Burgess arrived at the crime scene five minutes after they got the call. This time they were official, not undercover.

There was quite a lot of blood on the platform but, since the body was not on the track, the transport police had just taped off the area and temporarily closed the station. The body lay spread-eagled face down, the knife protruding from the small of her back.

'Did you check the cameras?' was Brewster's first question. Temporarily out of action, he was told.

Goddammit! He instantly lost his rag. He loathed such plodding incompetence. Did none of this crappy system ever work? What was the point of closed-circuit TV unless it bloody well functioned? he asked. The station official shrugged. These things happen.

The victim was slim and in very good shape; her phone was lying beside her. Brewster bagged it and handed it over. A police technician would rush it to the lab.

'Have you looked in her handbag?'

Not yet, he was told. They'd been waiting for Brewster to give the instruction. He slid on a pair of latex gloves and carefully opened the snakeskin bag: Chanel, he noted; presumably well off. He'd expected it to be empty. Her wallet, however, appeared untouched, and contained a hundred pounds in cash as well as a row of credit cards, one of them gold.

'Check her out,' he said to the team then followed Burgess back to the scene of the murder.

Mary Ellen Goddard (Meg to her friends) was a City banker from New York. She had worked in London for the past two years and rented a flat in the Bayswater Road, to which she had been returning when she was killed. She was on the phone to her boyfriend at the time, letting him know she was running late. He had started cooking when he took the call, and was now being treated for shock.

'What was the likely motivation?' Nothing appeared to have gone from her bag and she still had her Rolex watch and a pair of pearl earrings. She even carried her passport: not very wise.

Whatever the motive, she'd been struck so hard the blade

had severed her spinal cord. This was more than just a bungled mugging. It could be that she was followed from the bank, which was situated in Liverpool Street. So what was she doing at Baker Street, waiting for a train?

'Simple.' Brewster now knew his stuff, having done a crash course on the Circle Line. 'The train she didn't get on was Hammersmith bound.'

Which threw no light on who might have wanted to kill her. He made arrangements to talk to her boss and also the grief-stricken boyfriend, once he was up to it. Both knife and phone were now with forensics, though Brewster wasn't expecting much. The only prints they could ever match were those they already had on file and, so far, no modus operandi was apparent.

Brewster had digs in Meadow Road, a row of small houses by a council estate, close to the Oval cricket ground, handy for those rare occasions when he could snatch a few hours off. For the sake of convenience, since they worked as a team, Burgess was currently staying there too, which made things that much simpler. There was a park close by where they liked to stroll; stretching his legs helped to ease Brewster's pain and also focus his mind. There were kids on swings living normal lives; he would stand and watch them enjoying themselves and wonder where his own life went wrong and why his personal relationships didn't work out.

He had never been attracted to family life though realised now he'd have liked a son, one he could teach to bowl a googly or play guitar as well as Eric Clapton. One he'd have definitely headed off from getting involved with the police. Brewster's father had been a miner, granite-jawed and emotionally stunted, who had disapproved of his only son's progression to the SAS.

A waste of an education, was his view, an adult version of cops and robbers that would doubtless one day result in his premature death. But Brewster had never been much of a student, had veered towards cricket and playing the blues. His move into the SAS had been mainly a gesture of puerile rebellion.

But the active life had suited him; the danger had kept him on his toes. It had taken him all over the world where he'd picked up an alternative education; fluent Arabic and firearms training as well as surveillance work. A career that offered a constant challenge but had not equipped him for civilian life. At forty-two, his time was almost up. He had no idea what he'd do if forced to retire.

Nor was there anyone to share his life. He had made a point of travelling light, keeping himself emotionally free, perhaps the only way he could handle the job. In his youth he had played the field, yet always remained uncommitted. There were times he longed for a kindred spirit with whom to share his most intimate thoughts, his hopes and aspirations. Finch had been more than a working partner, had become his buddy and trusted friend. His death had left a hole in Brewster's life that he didn't expect to fill.

The second murder brought the nightmares back. He couldn't shake off the recurring image of that lifeless body in a pool of her own blood. The first might have been more graphically distressing but this one really drove home the point. That night he got out his easel and started to paint.

From charcoal sketches and watercolours he'd slowly progressed to using oils. Gone were the delicate well-observed touches; he found release in bold primal colours and violent images from his tortured subconscious. With a cigarette stuck in the corner of his mouth, he attacked the canvas with lethal fury in an effort to rid himself of the day's frustrations. By the time he stopped for a late-night drink, a hefty whisky to help him sleep, the band of tension inside his head was easing.

Two similar murders within a few days, both at stations on the Circle Line, with no attempt made to cover up the crime, at either end of the day. Both victims female and working for banks, though from entirely different backgrounds, east London and New York. Both in steady relationships. Both the boyfriends with alibis. Both struck in the back with considerable force by expensive finely honed knives. Both talking on their mobile phones at the time of the attack.

Two in five days might be bad enough but what they needed, to establish a pattern, was a third.

8

He was all fired up by the third time he killed. His palms were clammy, his heart rate fast. He had caught her so totally unawares, she hadn't had time to scream. He had chosen the knife with obsessive care, testing the blades till his fingers were bloodied. When he struck and felt it slide in, his reaction was almost orgasmic. At last he understood about life, was belatedly achieving his manhood.

He stayed around while they called the police; had nothing to fear having fixed the cameras before striking. There was only a dribble of people about, all intent on their own affairs. It was possible to be invisible if you tried. He'd inhaled her essence as he closed in, silently on his sneakered feet. Had she caught him watching, he'd have known how to reassure her.

Her various aromas had almost unnerved him, taking him back to much happier times. The cream, the powder, the expensive cloth, the gleam of the pearls against her skin. Somewhere inside his skull a prism had shattered. His choice of prey had been fairly random; this station was one of his hunting grounds. He had spent a couple of hours in the waxworks from which he found he could learn a lot. Then walked in the park and watched the young couples at their business. So much had been denied him all his life. Now it was his turn to get a piece of the action.

He had left at speed and picked out his quarry, alone on the station platform. She looked so serene in her chic pink suit as she chatted contentedly on her phone. He hated her china-doll prettiness, knew that he must have her.

The worst part was always the journey home, especially after she'd stayed on for drinks or someone had persuaded her out for a meal. Stage-door johnnies, her mother called them, refer-ring back to her own misspent youth, but Imogen only ever went out with people she already knew. Though she certainly had no shortage of invitations.

Since childhood she'd had it drummed into her never to take stupid risks or talk to strangers. Duncan had made her promise to call if she ever found herself stranded and in need of a lift. He could be there in twenty minutes, he said, since traffic at that hour was negligible. But Imogen felt that to call him would be wimpish, proof that she wasn't yet ready to live on her own. She loved being part of her mother's ménage but should soon be thinking of moving on. Alice and Julie seemed to have so much fun she was vaguely considering sharing with them. Alice had been suggesting it for some time. She was twenty-two, with her life before her. When the show closed, she'd have to sort something out.

Now, however, at the height of summer, it was worth the

journey to get home to Notting Hill. The house was spacious, she had a whole floor and few house rules to abide by. No noise after midnight was the paramount one. If she wanted company later than that, she just had to keep it down. No one she knew had parents like hers which was why she had little incentive to leave. But dancing at the National Theatre was widening her horizons.

The final curtain was at 10.35 and it took her at least twenty minutes to sort herself out. There were usually backstage visitors around which meant that, even if they weren't for her, she was often kept chatting at least for another half-hour. After that came the walk across the bridge which was usually still busy. She loved the spectacle of the river at night, with St Paul's Cathedral all lit up and the South Bank ablaze with its numerous busy venues. She had once been to Venice and liked that too but the Grand Canal was not nearly as grand as the Thames.

The last train home was at ten past twelve; Imogen usually caught it with ease. By that time most of the crowds had dispersed and only a handful of stalwarts remained, slumped in corners of carriages, often asleep. Occasionally there was a rowdy drunk but she'd grown adroit at avoiding them. The easiest way was to move to another carriage. Notting Hill felt immediately like home, the air there that much sweeter. She never felt threatened; she ran up the station steps with a lightening of heart. The streets were still busy and there was lots of traffic, and the two-minute walk home to Chepstow Villas had never bothered her at all.

Tonight she found her mother still up, with the weak excuse that they'd just got in and she'd been setting the breakfast table for the morning. She seemed relieved when Imogen arrived and gave her a long unnecessary hug.

'Mum,' said Imogen, 'I'm not a child. In five years I'll be the age you were when you had me.'

Beth simply laughed. 'Allow me,' she said, 'to worry about my baby girl if I want to.' She didn't mention the appalling newsflash, that another young woman had been stabbed to death on the Tube.

There was no one waiting up for him. When he got home in the early hours and crept up silently to his room, nothing stirred in the house. There was sometimes a light from beneath her door which probably meant she was sloshed again, but she never showed any concern for him or checked that he was all right. The first thing he needed to do was shower and rinse away the evening's excesses. He had travelled around on the Tube for hours, slowly coming down from his high.

He was still too aroused to be able to sleep so, draped in a towel, went down to plunder the fridge. She always kept it stocked with food, the very least she could do for him. There was ham and salami, half a cold chicken and a hunk of his favourite bread. He searched for the vodka but she must have got it upstairs. So he turned his attention to the well-stocked cellar and selected a bottle of finest claret, too good to squander like this but what the hell? He needed it; he was still unfulfilled as the thirst for danger grew stronger daily. She needled him with her chilly contempt. One of these days, if she didn't watch out, she was going to push him too far.

9

The shop had been Duncan's inspiration, created because he felt Beth was working too hard. It was ten years now since they'd got together but things had happened so fast it seemed far less. The catering business had been great fun but had meant her working relentless hours, which might have made sense as a single parent but not now. Wedding receptions and boardroom lunches had certainly kept the wolf from the door but divided her from her sexy new husband; not smart. Once they were married, which happened quite quickly, she never wanted him out of her sight and the trekking around and endless late nights had totally worn her out.

So, based on her tireless obsession with food, Duncan came up with his master plan. Situated in Marylebone High Street, flanked by an enclave of gourmet restaurants, the shop had become a magnet for foodies in search of ingredients they couldn't locate elsewhere. Palm hearts, pomegranates, chocolate truffles. A wide variety of cooking oils, and breads still warm and crusty from the oven. It was a feast for the senses from the moment it opened, and right up until they closed the shutters they did a very brisk trade. 'The Food Emporium.' That said it all. Word spread rapidly; the columnists gave it high marks.

At first Beth found standing all day a strain but soon got herself into shape. She and Duncan would jog round the park, rising at dawn in the summer months and still creeping out when the winter mornings closed in. Hyde Park was only a stone's throw away, as well as the mansions of Palace Gardens Terrace where oil sheikhs and football moguls now had their homes. They loved to wander down the gated street, towards the palace full of minor royals, then on to Kensington High Street, bustling with shoppers.

'Happy?' he'd ask as he squeezed her hand.

'Deliriously so,' she'd reply.

'Whatever happened to Vivienne?' asked Jane, still Beth's closest, most enduring friend. 'Do you keep in touch? I don't hear her mentioned these days.'

'We swap Christmas cards,' Beth said guardedly. 'And her cats are still registered with the practice.' Duncan saw her at least once a year, when her pampered darlings came in for their jabs, but no longer bothered to mention it when he did. That episode of Beth's life was closed; she wasn't proud of her out-of-wedlock liaison. But she hadn't, of course, known Vivienne then, her sole excuse for the way she'd behaved; also Duncan had not yet entered her life.

'And Georgy?'

'Occasionally. She's a loyal friend. She was here for the opening of *Anything Goes*.'

Georgy, another name from the past, these days was really more Imogen's friend. She tracked her career with genuine interest and spoilt her whenever she could. She had started off as a dancer herself before moving on to photography. These days she ran a photo gallery in the meat-packing district of New York.

'Did she ever marry?'

'Not so far,' said Beth. Georgy had carried a torch for her own ex.

'What is she – forty?'

'Younger,' said Beth. 'Mid to late thirties, and I must say she still looks great.'

A whole decade. Could it be that long? So much had happened since then to them all, yet the memories still remained fresh as well as painful. Beth felt she was now a different person; older, maybe, but also much wiser. She had never been tempted, since her happy second marriage, to so much as glance at anyone else. The house, the business, her beloved daughter. She had them all, plus the man she adored. Fate had been kind to Beth; she was content.

Not so Celeste, bitter and sad, for whom just waking was an ordeal. She had spent the whole of her life in this house and in just a few years would be forty. Yet all she had to show for it were the lines of disappointment etched into her face and a mouth that was hardening into a narrow line. Once she'd been fêted for her startling looks; the photo albums downstairs bore witness to that. The child of a famous theatrical pair, Sir Edward Forrester and Esmée Morell, she had always taken it for granted she'd follow in their footsteps.

Esmée Morell was the darling of her age, undisputed queen

of the London stage. Famed for her wit and vivacity, her per-formances had always been sell-outs. Even at fifty, she was offered the starriest roles. Her marriage, too, was legendary; they had played together in the *Dream* at Stratford. She was well into her thirties by then but he had stopped her in her tracks.

'All it took was a single glance,' she never tired of boasting. 'God knows, by then I'd been in and out of love as regularly as the swing doors of a pub. But when dearest Teddy appeared, that was it for us both.'

He was slightly camp, which was part of his charm, and a stunningly handsome man. Tall and distinguished as a diplomat, he towered over his fragile wife who was, in reality, tough as old boots, though careful never to show it. He towered, she gushed; they were made for each other. No one else, not even their children, got so much as a look in.

Celeste no longer looked at the pictures; they were locked away to keep her from further pain. For eighteen years she had hogged the limelight until, without warning, the music had stopped. It was over, though the world never knew what had happened. People had offered her money to talk but she main-tained a resolute silence. Those days were dead, which was no bad thing. The older she grew, the more she saw how warped her childhood had been and how corrosive. There were still some questions that needed answers but she'd put it all in the past. They'd imprisoned her in a living tomb from which she would never get out.

Rupert's idea for a TV series was hardly revolutionary but the faded cuttings he had thrown together immediately had Julie hooked. *Theatrical Legends* was the working title, to be aimed at a mass television audience, primarily in the States. He'd included a handful of obvious names – Valentino, James Dean and Garbo – along with a handful less well known whom Julie had not even heard of. Her role as researcher was to flesh out their lives and try to fill in any gaps. This was the sort of project she loved, which could prove more fun than her regular work. The gossip angle attracted her and a TV credit would look good on her CV.

Tonight she had brought the folders home since the office was not conducive to much concentration. She lay in bed and flicked through the contents, instantly absorbed. The more she read, the more involved she became. She knew little about the London theatre, having grown up in a celluloid age, and her Yorkshire childhood had not included culture. Actors, to her, meant movie stars; she had never even seen a Shakespeare play. But *Theatrical Legends* had caught her fancy; starting with Sarah Bernhardt, she was hooked.

It was almost like a detective series; some of the cases were particularly intriguing. It amazed her how many big stars simply dropped out of sight. Lauren Bacall was occasionally in the news but Gloria Grahame had faded right out and spent her final days in a Liverpool slum.

'Who on earth was Esmée Morell?' she'd asked Rupert, never having encountered the name before.

'Esmée Morell and Edward Forrester were titans of their age,' he said. 'In their day as famous as the Redgraves are now.'

'So how come I've never heard of them?'

'Neither ever made a film. They were thespians in the grand old style, adored by the theatre-going public.'

'Why are they on this list?' asked Julie.

'They died within a few weeks of each other, both still at the height of their fame. For no known reason, it appears to have been hushed up. It is up to you to try to find out why.'

Her eyes grew heavy; it was time for sleep. It was ten minutes after midnight. She'd devote her weekends to the bulk of the work, which Rupert was keen to get finished fast. Tomorrow she'd draw up a list of old films and order the DVDs. She had always been a movie buff; the project was right up her street. She stuffed the cuttings back into their folders and stacked the lot on the bedside table. A monochrome photograph fluttered out and she checked the back to see who it was: a wasp-waisted beauty in a cartwheel hat covered in ostrich feathers. Nobody Julie recognised. Though the pose looked Edwardian, the date was 1979.

Esmée Morell, the caption read. *Playing the lead in Pygmalion. Opposite her husband, Edward Forrester.*

10

Kimberley Martin was from Walthamstow. Brewster went down there alone. The streets were anonymous, like his own part of town; it took him a good ten minutes to find the house. Despite the heat, all the curtains were closed; an obvious place of mourning. He felt apologetic for his intrusion. The mother showed him into the lounge; the father, who worked on the buses, had gone in to work. Her eyes were puffy and red from weeping. She offered him tea which he declined. He would not take up much of her time, he said, awkwardly patting her shoulder. It was the part of the job that he liked the least but something that had to be done.

Had Kimberley any dubious friends? The questions were purely routine. Was it possible she could have been in some sort of trouble?

No. Her mother was adamant. Kim had always been a very good girl, just promoted at work and with excellent prospects.

The interview took less than an hour; he could see he was adding to her distress. At least they had managed to keep the newshounds at bay. He scribbled some notes then left her to it, inadequate in the face of such grief. What sort of a world was this? He often wondered.

Next on his list was the banker's boss. He wasn't expecting more luck there but it should be less distressing. Brewster sighed as he walked to the car. He hated the suffering of innocent people. On occasions like this he could wish himself back in the battle-zones of Iraq.

As he drove through the grimy congested streets, he contemplated the teeming masses that make up the colourful sprawl of London's East End, sanctuary to all kinds of refugees who, over the centuries, learned to live together, respecting each other's beliefs and embracing their cultures. Only a very few dissidents, fired by prejudice or warped beliefs, occasionally rocked the boat with violent behaviour. There were eight million people in Greater London, considerably swelled at this time of year by tourists. And among those masses was a frenzied killer who'd committed two murders in less than a week.

Back at his easel later that night, Brewster ran through in his mind where they'd got so far. Two nasty murders, five days apart, both young women talking on their phones. Both, as it happened, working for banks. Both on the Circle Line. There had been a report of an accidental death, again a woman in the rush hour crowd. Although there had been no suggestion of murder, it fitted the same MO. She too had been using her phone. Could there be some connection?

The painting he'd started was rapidly growing as he slashed and stabbed at the canvas. He had chosen colours that were garish and bright, in some places harsh on the eye. They helped release a force within him that assuaged the anger in his soul. Red for blood and the carnage on the track; purple and indigo for violent death. Even the evenings were growing shorter as the summer seeped away. Scarlet and black for Finch's head as the booby trap blew him to smithereens.

A final whisky before he turned in. Nevertheless, he would probably not sleep.

11

Much to Margaret's irritation, the colours were not precisely right. The dyes were obviously from a different batch. It would mean another trek into town, the last thing she really wanted to do. The garden needed her full attention; it was her memorial to Jack. But the work on the den was almost complete; all that remained to be done was that dratted last cushion. The weather was glorious so she'd give herself a treat and turn the chore into a proper day out. She checked the listings to see what was on and decided the time had come to visit the Globe. She had read a lot about what they had done. Today, while there wasn't a cloud in the sky, seemed ideal for watching an open-air performance. She booked a ticket for the matinée – *The Winter's Tale*, a play she didn't know. It was scheduled to end around twenty to five which meant she could comfortably catch her train home before the worst of the evening rush hour started. She thought about asking a friend along but could think of no one likely to be free whose company she could bear for so many hours. Haywards Heath was nice enough but hardly overflowing with kindred spirits. She had lost her dearest friend when her husband died.

To fit in the wool shop before the show she would have to start making tracks right away. She picked out a neat linen lavender two-piece that Jack had always particularly liked, and a pair of sensible flat-heeled shoes for a leisurely stroll along the river. Her spirits had risen by the time she set off. She was suddenly looking forward to the jaunt.

It was the Diefenbakers' last day in London; they still had lots to fit in. Ellie felt quite wrung out after Hampton Court. Though dying for a chance to look at the shops, she had meekly followed where Wilbur led; had looked at enough old buildings to last a lifetime. Today they were heading to Parliament Square and, after that, on to County Hall to see the aquarium and ride on the London Eye. Ellie, who had no head for heights, would sooner remain on terra firma but knew from experience that Wilbur would simply not listen. They only ever did what he wanted. She had given up arguing long ago.

So 'Yes, dear' she murmured, praying for rain. Treacherous, maybe, but at least it might get her to Harrods.

But the sun blazed forth and the tourists swarmed. He made her walk across Westminster Bridge after they'd had a whistle-stop tour of the Abbey. She was only grateful that Parliament wasn't in session. By the time they arrived at County Hall, Ellie was virtually dropping. She would kill for a coffee and a nice sit down but Wilbur was striding in front, as always, and before she knew it they were passing through the turnstile.

The aquarium was impressive, she couldn't deny it, though

she'd never really had much time for fish except when served with hollandaise sauce and some lovely crispy French fries. Which reminded her how hungry she was; they'd been at it all morning, with no time for lunch, and it would, when they'd done the Eye, be well after four.

'Come along,' said Wilbur briskly. 'Don't start flagging now. There'll be time enough for napping on Eurostar.'

The new Globe Theatre was fabulous, an exact reconstruction of how it had been when Shakespeare was alive. Since the actual performance didn't start till two, Margaret went round the exhibition to get her into a suitable mood for the play. She was glad she had come. The weather was perfect, and she was feeling quite light-hearted. Her one regret was not having Jack there to share it. As students they regularly queued for the Old Vic; she'd seen numerous fine performances there, including the young Richard Burton in his heyday.

The seats were narrow and had no backs which meant she had to concentrate, though she still found it hard to understand the play. She took a break and wandered outside to eat an ice cream and look at the boats, then strolled back just in time for the second half. She liked the authentic informality, though in Shakespeare's day they'd have eaten oranges, not ice cream. Or was that Nell Gwynn? Margaret really didn't know. To her relief, the final act turned into a bit of a pantomime, with everyone singing and dancing and getting married.

Margaret, her spirits now fully restored, spilled out into the street with the rest and started retracing her steps towards Waterloo station. She lingered awhile beneath a bridge to thumb through the tables of second-hand books. This stretch of the river was reminiscent of the left bank of the Seine. Further along, close to the National Theatre, there were acrobats and high-wire artists performing bravely in front of an eddying crowd. She'd have liked to stay longer but checked her watch. She didn't want to miss her five o'clock train.

Along the river living statues posed. A clown, an angel, a Tutankhamen, all of them showing no sign of life to a quite disconcerting degree. They might be clever but they spooked her slightly. She had an urge to creep up and say boo, to check just how good their reflexes really were. At the flick of a coin, they would break the pose and make an elaborate bow. The Tutankhamen was especially good; she stopped for a moment to study him. His face was concealed by a golden mask that had a fixed expression. It was a curious way to earn a living. Why couldn't he get more regular work? Having raised two children, she did not really approve.

She longed to stop for a cup of tea, even though it meant cutting things very fine. Then she remembered that no one was waiting at home; she need not hurry back. She could stay on in town for as long as she liked and catch a later train. Her car was safely parked at the station and no one ever got mugged in Haywards Heath. But her heart wasn't in it; she had had her day out, and the gnawing grief was setting in again. She decided, after all, to call it a day.

There was much activity on the South Bank as Wilbur and Ellie shoved their way through to buy their tickets for the London Eye then join the endless queue. Wilbur, at last taking pity on her, told her to go and sit under the trees and buy herself whatever she liked from the kiosk. So she bought a coffee and a chocolate bar and settled comfortably on a bench; a minor triumph that made her feel heaps better. With the weight off her feet, her spirits rose; at last she had time to relax and look around. She loved this city, despite its size, regretted now that they had to move on. Just as she was growing acclimatised, he was whisking her off to Paris.

There was street entertainment all along the river, with a jazz band playing quite close to her. She relaxed in the sunshine and waved to Wilbur, making slow progress along the queue. Her eyelids started to droop so she closed them. She was, after all, on vacation.

Once he became aware of them, they seemed to be everywhere, solitary women of every age, wistfully searching, he felt, for something undefined. He detected a sadness in their eyes that matched the emptiness of his soul, a gnawing hunger for something he'd not yet achieved. Standing here, as he often did, he studied them as they wandered past, aimlessly, with nowhere specific to go. Since that first sharp thrill he was hungry for more, on the alert for another easy target, growing increasingly restless each time he struck. No need to stick with the young and brash. A door in his memory opened a crack and he glimpsed, for a second, the past he tried hard to suppress.

A woman in lavender paused to look, fair and pretty in a faded way, her mind clearly set on other things; in no particular hurry. She was roughly the age that *she* must have been then, the day when his world crashed around him.

A flash of sunlight, a flurry of commotion, an arc of blood, as the blade went in, that had spattered his face and matted his hair; he recalled the rusty smell. For a second he felt himself growing faint as his hands went clammy and his heartbeat quickened, but he managed to steady himself before he fell. He felt the urge coming on again, a strong compulsion that made him shake. He tensed his muscles and focused on keeping his balance. No matter what, he must not lose control. He took deep breaths till the panic attack had subsided.

Someone was watching. Ellie woke with a start and sat up quickly in case Wilbur wanted her. But there he stood, still in the queue, having only advanced about twenty yards. She waved to him gaily and he waved back. She still had that feeling of eyes upon her though when she turned to look there was no one there. A tremor of fear shuddered down her spine. She gathered her things in a bit of a hurry and went to stand beside Wilbur.

The ride was better than she had expected. The wheel seemed hardly to move at all. And there was enough room in the glassed-in pod to allow you to walk around. The panorama spread beneath them took in a large part of Greater London. The higher they went, the wider the view. Ellie, forgetting her fear of heights, squealed as she recognised places.

'Look!' she cried. 'There's Buckingham Palace.' And the Houses of Parliament close to them. And the river, winding like a silver ribbon past Canary Wharf and the Isle of Dogs and down to Hampton Court in the other direction. Wilbur took loads of photographs with his new and expensive digital camera. He'd have endless enjoyment for the rest of the year, boring them all with his picture shows.

After the apex came the slow descent, gliding smoothly down towards County Hall. As the pod moved gradually closer to the ground, the wheel continued its ceaseless motion. A couple of uniformed guards stood by to help the passengers get off.

'Here, love, give me your hand,' said one and Ellie stepped daintily on to the platform, assuming Wilbur was following right behind her. Later it wasn't quite clear how it happened; perhaps he was too engrossed with his camera, but, right at the very last moment, he stumbled and fell.

'Whoa, there,' said the uniformed official. 'Take it easy, old chap.' He tried to catch him but Wilbur was heavy. His bulk almost flattened the man.

It could have turned out to be really nasty, but one of the guards pressed the button and stopped the wheel.

'Are you all right, sir?' He tried to help but Wilbur was scrambling back to his feet, annoyed at making such a fool of himself in public.

'Absolutely,' he said abruptly, waving the fellow away. Leaning heavily on Ellie's shoulder he limped along the walkway to the steps then, slowly and painfully, made his way down to the ground.

He stood for a moment, testing his balance, then slowly crumpled like a building collapsing and sprawled across the footpath, unable to rise.

Margaret, passing and seeing it happen, swiftly stepped forward and offered her hand. 'I trained as a nurse,' she explained to Ellie. Then, when he failed to get back on his feet, she advised him to lie there and not try to move. 'Wait while I summon the ambulance people.'

It didn't look awfully good.

12

When obliged to drop out of drama school, Celeste's only option was to look for a job. She had no other training, could not even type; all that was going for her were her looks and some timeless couturier clothes. She tried to sign up with a model agency but was told she was too small for the catwalk, though they'd try to get her some advertising work. The money wasn't great but kept them alive. The outlook was fairly bleak though at least they had a substantial roof over their heads. When her parents died, they left almost nothing, had given the future little thought. Celeste's whole life was, in theory, mapped out. They just hadn't paid her RADA fees, though had luckily left the house in trust for the boy.

Esmée had been a gigantic snob which was where the bulk of the money had gone. Never saved, just frittered away on cocktail parties, designer clothes, tickets for Glyndebourne, Ascot outings and lavish house parties in the south of France.

The Tite Street house was a social hub where only the well connected were welcome. Rich or famous, preferably both; her address book bulged with illustrious names she could drop. She had passed this snobbery on to her daughter who baulked at the thought of a suitor who wasn't top drawer. At eighteen she could have had her pick; the heir to a dukedom, a baronet or two. She had turned up her nose at them all.

The shock of losing both parents at once had thrown Celeste temporarily off balance. For a while her future looked very dicey but she had no choice but to soldier on. Someone had to put food on the table; her brother, at the time, was only eight. When the advertising work fizzled out, she got a job in a department store, demonstrating sewing machines and, later, Kenwood mixers. It might not be acting but did draw a crowd; the personnel people were pleased. But she quickly grew irritated by mindless shoppers asking the same dumb questions all the time while their husbands tried to grope her. She packed it in and went back to reading the job ads.

The post of receptionist filled the bill, as much as anything could do. At least she got to wear her nice clothes and to work in a classier part of town. Her inborn snobbery had not reduced one bit. Dr Rousseau was heavily French, with elaborate Gallic good manners. He was suave and silky, as befitted his profession, and appreciated her glamorous looks. The five-storey house was split up into suites with a different surgeon on every landing, each with his own backup staff, and a general administration team on the ground floor. It was decorated in muted good taste in keeping with the fees they charged. Celeste, not given to casual small talk, was on nodding terms with the other employees, mainly women of quiet refinement doing parallel jobs. Now and again she had lunch with one but they never

70

particularly hit it off. She couldn't help letting her attitude show, that she found such employment demeaning. But it covered the bills and got her out of the house.

Beth occasionally saw her in the street, wandering aimlessly in her lunch hour, sometimes pausing outside the shop as if thinking of venturing in. Beth resolved that, if she ever did, she would boldly introduce herself. Something about the stranger's bleakness touched and also intrigued her. Though rarely out of sorts herself, Beth recognised a tormented soul. Her clothes were classic, her jewellery minimal, she seemed never to have a hair out of place. Yet among the crowds in Marylebone High Street, she always looked totally lost. She reminded Beth vaguely of a woman she'd known with whom she had shared a traumatic experience. Vivienne Nugent, a society beauty, had had that same look of suppressed despair, despite the expensive and pampered life she led. These days they only rarely met, though once they had been good friends.

Which was why Beth was drawn to this younger woman, based on a feeling of unresolved guilt. Friendship became more precious as one grew older. And since their paths appeared destined to cross, she would take that first step and introduce herself.

The curse of beauty was underrated. Celeste saw proof of that every day. In they came, troubled and insecure, malcontents chasing a cherished dream, convinced that whatever was wrong in their lives could be fixed by a surgeon's knife. Now and then it was worth what it cost, as with the deb with the overlarge nose, hoping to be transformed by the time of her ball. But mostly they simply deluded themselves by assuming that beauty was the ultimate prize. Celeste knew only too well how wrong that was. Had she been able to turn back time, these days she'd choose to be ordinary but happy. Her sensational looks had brought her only disappointment. She'd been set apart from an early age, since other girls only envied her and boys were too scared to try to chat her up. The admirers she had dismissed with scorn had gone on to marry plainer girls, while she was still on her own with no one to love her.

Nobody noticed her any more, except the occasional randy old man, and the patients who looked at her with detachment. The desolation of her private life was known to only a few. Because of her situation, she had no friends. She had many times thought of running away but the burden her parents had landed her with could not be abandoned because she had a conscience. For years she'd assumed that her prince would one day come and carry her off on his milk-white steed. That dream had long been locked away with the photos.

Julie was full of her television project which was taking increasingly more of her time. The deeper she delved, the more enthralling it became. She brought home videos and DVDs and Alice would order a takeaway while they sat up late with a bottle of wine soaking themselves in old films.

'This is loads more fun than reading,' said Alice, who usually had her nose in a book and hardly ever went to the pictures at all. 'I confess I've missed out on most of these classic movies.'

'Which is why Rupert dreamt it up. The series is aimed at people like you who don't know your Garbo from your elbow.'

When Imogen dropped in after Sunday lunch, having walked from home to stretch her legs, she was startled to find them both slumped in semi-darkness. 'What in the world are you watching?' she asked, plonking herself on the sofa beside them. She removed her sneakers to allow her toes to breathe.

'*Hangover Square*,' said Julie abstractedly, busily scribbling notes.

'Linda Darnell is on her list,' Alice explained, making room for her. The kettle was boiling; she was about to make a pot of tea.

'I've always fancied George Sanders,' said Imogen, 'though shouldn't you both be outside on a day like this?'

'You are starting to sound like your mother,' said Alice, laughing.

Out of deference to Imogen, they switched the film off and Julie produced a bottle of wine. 'Drink?' she asked, with corkscrew poised.

'Please,' said Imogen. 'I really shouldn't but, what the hell, it's Sunday.'

'Thank God for people who drink,' muttered Julie. Alice and her perpetual tea. She was secretly slightly in awe of Imogen and wanted the chance to get to know her better. Stardom thrilled her to her Yorkshire roots; she had never encountered a professional dancer before.

'I can't believe you walked all that way. Shouldn't you be relaxing at home?' Julie never took exercise at all if she could help it.

'It's part of a dancer's daily regime and walking through the park is more fun than just doing basic stretching.'

Julie told her about her project and Imogen was intrigued. She found all aspects of show business fascinating.

'Who are the people you're doing?' she asked. Julie passed her the list. Imogen skimmed it and, just like them both, stopped

73

at the name of Esmée Morell, one she didn't know at all; odd since it was her profession.

'She's the one who interests me most,' said Julie, handing her the photographs. 'Most of the others are fairly straightforward but with her I keep drawing blanks.'

Imogen studied the pictures closely. 'She was certainly very pretty,' she said. 'I tell you what, why not come backstage and talk to some of the cast? You never know. It's a very small world.'

'Thanks,' said Julie, secretly thrilled. 'She's the one I am finding the hardest. And my deadline is creeping closer.'

'What happened to her?' asked Imogen, curious. Normally things like that were easily looked up.

'Nobody knows, which is why she's included. That's the main thrust of the series.'

'Do you have her on DVD?' asked Imogen. 'I'd really like to see her in action.'

'No,' said Julie. 'That's the crazy part. She never appeared on the screen.'

'So why is she in the series at all?'

'In her day she was a colossal stage star who seemingly vanished overnight. Nobody knows what happened.'

13

Brewster and Burgess were back on the beat, patrolling the Circle Line. The tourist invasion had reached its peak; the trains were stifling, with too many passengers sweating and swearing as tempers stretched and frayed. It was no way to travel at this time of year; even a dog would rebel.

Methodically they checked every carriage, taking the occasional break to sit and study the fluctuating crowd. Observation, Brewster knew, was vital to the surveillance process. The traffic flow at different stations was something he now understood. At the major ones, like King's Cross and Victoria, they lingered longer and were more alert. Burgess's expertise was bombs; Brewster cared more about human interaction.

As he idly watched Burgess doing his stuff, minutely examining every seat, Brewster pondered the criminal mind, specifically what might trigger the actions of a psychopathic killer. Take, for instance, a woman on her phone. Raised voices drew

75

immediate attention though a whisper could have the same effect. Someone speaking *sotto voce* gives the impression of having something to hide. It is only human nature to want to eavesdrop.

But where to start looking, he had no idea. What they badly needed was another lead. Though it was hardly kosher to wish for another murder.

Gradually there were certain people whose faces started to strike a chord. Since most commuters keep regular hours, a pattern slowly began to form of who was travelling from A to B at what time. Not everyone would make that connection; Brewster was specially trained. Several times they encountered the busker who clearly had his own regular patch. The policeman in Brewster wondered if he had bothered to get himself a licence. He also saw several homeless people who seemed to spend the whole day on the Tube, most of them fast asleep or else heavily drugged.

They took their breaks at different stops to vary their observation points. They even occasionally rose to street level and walked for a couple of blocks.

Off duty, Brewster listened to jazz or drifted down to the local pub to sit in the corner with a couple of beers, absorbing the atmosphere. The way to know a community was to act invisible and simply listen. This pub was basic, all spit and sawdust, with excellent ale and a dartboard always in use. Women occasionally came on to him but Brewster hadn't a problem with that. A cop couldn't really stay undercover without attracting a degree of interest and his vanity, though in some ways dented, on that score remained intact. At times he ached for some human contact but was not yet ready to socialise. He came here partly for relaxation but also for basic research.

He wondered, as he so often had, what motivated a person to kill and if that something could then turn into a habit. He had many times been in the line of fire but only ever in the course of duty. The few occasions he had pulled the trigger had been strict emergencies. But that was war, for which he'd been trained. He'd been fighting for a justified cause. The solitary chancer, acting alone, was another matter entirely. This one appeared to be doing it for kicks, knowing there was an even chance he'd be caught.

Brewster studied his fellow drinkers, all of them, except him, in friendly groups. Did it take a loner to be a killer or could they ever lead ordinary lives? The Yorkshire Ripper had a wife who had sworn she knew nothing about his crimes.

Time to leave. It was getting late. His brain functioned best when he'd had sufficient sleep.

14

It was several hours later, well into rush hour. Margaret had stuck around in case she could help. Wilbur had been taken to St Thomas' Hospital, only yards away; the stretcher had arrived in minutes. She sat with Ellie in the cafeteria, awaiting the doctor's verdict. She hadn't the heart to abandon her at such a time.

'We're supposed to move on to Paris tomorrow.' Ellie was scared and unable to cope, unused to having to make decisions herself. She sipped at the coffee Margaret had bought her, twisting her handkerchief in distress.

'Wait till you hear what they have to say. It could be that he's OK after all. It was a nasty tumble but he may be no more than bruised.'

Privately, though, she was not convinced. She had seen the awkward way he had fallen and feared this might be the start of far worse to come.

'Tell me about yourself,' she said, tactfully trying to change the subject. The Diefenbakers were from the Midwest which was all she knew so far. Ellie was wearing a velvet jacket over a printed cotton dress, with a cameo brooch at her throat like a much older woman. But a paperback by Anita Shreve was peeking out of her bag, which suggested her clothes belied her taste in fiction. A pretty woman when she wasn't so fraught, with delicate bones and a clear, almost girlish, complexion.

At first she was at a loss for words. Her eyes flickered nervously round the room, awaiting the summons that never seemed to come. 'They are certainly taking their time,' she fretted. 'It doesn't look very good.'

Margaret explained about the NHS, that it had been greatly maligned. The waiting lists were incredibly long but in a matter of urgency, like this, they were able to streamline things fast. She refrained from adding that, in the States, they wouldn't have picked Wilbur up off the street until they'd seen proof that he had sufficient insurance. Nothing like that had been mentioned here. They had lifted him carefully on to the stretcher and admitted him straight away.

Gradually Ellie loosened up and ceased her endless fidgeting. Again she remembered how famished she was so Margaret went to get her a sausage roll. She was in the queue when a woman appeared, carrying a clipboard and looking for Ellie. As soon as she found her, she led her away and Margaret promised to wait. She was hungry too but would stick around until she was certain this poor lost soul was properly taken care of.

Wilbur's hip was severely fractured; they were going to have to keep him in. It seemed bizarre that a simple fall could have caused so much damage. There was nothing that Ellie could do for a while; he was under heavy sedation and the doctors were waiting to have a look at his X-rays.

'If you come back around ten,' said the nurse, 'we should be able to give you more information.'

There was a noisy bistro at Waterloo station in which Margaret had eaten several times. It was always packed with after-work drinkers, plus the early pre-theatre crowd, but the food was good and the service friendly and, very quickly, the noise level dropped as the tables began to clear. They found one in a distant corner and Margaret immediately ordered a bottle of wine.

'I think you could do with a drink,' she said, ignoring Ellie's feeble protests. The American woman was in shock and could do with a bit of a booster.

Ellie was not a habitual drinker but the Sauvignon Blanc helped to steady her nerves and the menu on the blackboard was very enticing.

'If you're really hungry,' suggested Margaret, 'you couldn't do better than the bouillabaisse.' And when Ellie didn't know what that was, she described it.

Ellie was cautious. It sounded very foreign, but she did like fish and was now completely famished. 'If you think I should,' she said cautiously, so Margaret summoned the waitress and ordered it twice. She had given up hope of that early train so, provided she didn't leave it too late, was now resigned to an evening in town in one of her favourite eateries. She topped up their glasses then settled back to try to get to know her new friend better.

*   *   *

The obvious place to start was the Internet but Julie had little success with that. There were references to the Forresters but only in listings, without any personal details. A chronology of their leading roles (they'd been especially busy in the fifties and sixties when Esmée, especially, had been the toast of both London and New York) but, frustratingly, nothing about their private lives.

'Where else can I look?' she wailed to Rupert, hating to seem such a useless wimp, ashamed at being unseated at the first fence.

'Don't ask me, duckie,' was his caustic reply, as he concentrated on today's review of last night's disastrous opening. 'What do you think I am paying you for? Now run along, dear, and stop interrupting my muse.'

He was right; she shouldn't have bothered him. In her lunch hour she slipped across to the library and immersed herself in the theatre section, hoping to be enlightened. Not much there either; just volumes of reviews with occasional mentions of Esmée in the footnotes, mainly giving only chapter and verse of roles in which she had starred. The fact that she'd married Edward Forrester was also scarcely alluded to. A veil seemed to have been drawn over both of them.

Julie returned to the *Daily Mail* and, on an impulse, phoned Imogen who, she knew, was usually home at that time. With nothing to do.

Imogen, idly painting her nails and watching a vapid Australian soap, was only too delighted to be interrupted. Julie outlined her problem and Imogen thought.

'She must have performed at the NT,' she said. 'Everyone who was anyone did so in those days. Let me talk to the folks backstage, some of whom have been there for yonks, and see what they can come up with.'

She had nothing to do till that evening's performance so would get there early and nose around. She was growing tired of being idle; it was good to have something to do.

Margaret stayed as long as she dared, then dropped Ellie back at the hospital before taking the taxi on to Victoria station. She wrote down her number before she left, wished Ellie luck and urged her to stay in touch.

'Call any time and I really mean it,' she said as she hugged her goodbye. Their meal together had been a success; she had really enjoyed their conversation once Ellie was over the initial shock and able to turn her mind to other things. With a couple of glasses of wine inside her, she'd revealed a bright and intelligent wit. When she talked about life in Chippewa Falls, a wicked glint came into her eyes. She made it sound quite a lot like Haywards Heath. Despite the fact she had lived there all her life and was therefore a fixture in the town, she confessed she'd never quite felt she fitted in. Church affairs, jam-making and such were all very well when the children were small but these days, now they had both left home, she found more and more that she needed some space. The worst thing that could have happened was her husband's retirement.

'I like to read and Wilbur does not. And now he is constantly under my feet. I don't mind admitting I miss the days when he was away at the office.'

Margaret laughed. The complaint rang bells though she'd never had any such problem with Jack. They'd had so much in common; she missed him badly.

'How long has it been?' asked Ellie softly, gently patting her hand. She could see the unnatural brightness of Margaret's eyes.

'Almost a year now,' Margaret told her, taking out a tissue and blowing her nose.

'There is nothing to beat a good marriage,' said Ellie. 'And at least you still have your children.'

Margaret pulled a face which made Ellie laugh. She told Margaret about the classes she took in renaissance history and visual arts. It meant a lot of essay writing but she managed to fit it all in.

'My husband thinks I'm quite mad,' she said. 'But as long as he gets his meals on time, he graciously allows me to do my own thing. Only in my own time, of course. Running the house comes first.'

Margaret was impressed as well as surprised that this quiet woman had such an internal life. It made her feel guilty that all she did now was loll around on the sofa and read, or listen to music and plays on Radio 4. The garden was really her only hobby; she ought to get into London more. With a friend like Ellie, with similar tastes, she would make it a regular thing.

Much as she would have loved to stay, she really had to catch that train. As it was she only just made it in time to the station.

15

The hotel desk clerk, whose name was Tom, could not have been more sympathetic. He had no problem with extending Ellie's stay and also offered to exchange their tickets and explain the situation to the travel people. There was no reason why the tickets to Paris should not be transferred to a later date.

'I assume you do have insurance,' he said but Ellie confessed that she didn't know. Wilbur always took care of details like that.

She tried not to panic. He was in safe hands and the doctors assured her that, all going well, he should make a complete recovery. She wasn't sure what to tell the family, though Monday was Independence Day and she'd have to make a call and talk to them then. She decided to play it down a bit in case one of her sons-in-law should fly over, which would be even worse than just having Wilbur to contend with. Now that she'd found a kindred spirit, Ellie was getting a whiff of freedom, which she liked.

She went to see him, in a public ward with his leg slung up on a special harness like an exhibit in the Natural History Museum. It was Saturday morning; according to their schedule they should by now have been en route to Paris. She brought him a pile of magazines though, throughout their marriage, he had never been much of a reader. He mainly just skimmed the financial news before devouring the sporting pages. A typical man, or so she privately thought.

'I've a good mind to sue,' were his opening words. 'As soon as they let me out of here, I intend to call my lawyer.'

'Yes, dear,' said Ellie in her dutiful way, only now starting to comprehend that they had her tyrannical husband a virtual prisoner. She even had to fetch him a bedpan because he wasn't allowed to move. The nurse said he would be in for at least three weeks.

After a while he told Ellie to go; he had never had much of an attention span and his wife's doleful face was starting to grate on his nerves.

'Don't just sit there,' he growled at her. 'Take advantage of the money we're wasting. There's no point hanging around in that dismal hotel.' He warned her, though, to watch her spending and to keep a careful note of everything. London was an expensive city; the much looked-forward-to trip was a total disaster.

Back in the street, having done her duty, Ellie had nothing she needed to do. The sky was clouding, and it looked like rain. The last thing she felt like was walking. She could either trek back to Waterloo or cross the bridge to the Underground. A taxi approached so she flagged it down.

'Harrods,' she told the driver.

* . * . *

He remembered little about his early childhood except that certain aspects stood out in sharp relief because of the echoing silence. The house was vast, like a mausoleum, except on the nights when the world flocked in and all the doors were flung open to welcome the guests and their hangers-on. In the two main reception rooms the rugs were removed and the floors wax-polished for the dancing, while the curtains were taken down and steam-cleaned then carefully rehung. The brass and silver were vigorously polished and the huge chandeliers sprayed with gin. An army of florists spent whole days garlanding every room.

They came in their hundreds, the great and not so good; actresses, barristers, politicians. Stars from every branch of the performing arts. Occasionally even minor royalty; she had been adept at sucking up and the hint of a title was enough to get her fawning. The fires with their scented logs were lit and myriad candles flickered. A string quartet played discreetly from above.

The children, of course, were banished upstairs but watched the proceedings from the darkened landing until an irritable nursery maid chivvied them off to bed. They saw the visitors milling beneath in their sumptuous clothes and exquisite jewellery until the moment a hush descended and the hostess made her grand entrance. She was fond of hats, even in her own home; they added some grandeur to her tiny person and accentuated the delicacy of her features. Hats and gloves were her signature note, with tightly laced boots to show off her legs. She gushed and gleamed and fluttered her fingers, smiling coquettishly at the crowd until someone encouraged her to give them a song and she took up her place at the piano.

Which was when her daughter would be summoned down and together they'd sing a cute duet, the child immaculate in virginal white with socks to match and highly polished shoes.

He would kneel and watch them doing their stuff, the candlelight gleaming on his sister's hair as she pranced and performed as outrageously as her mother. The little snob. Then all the ladies would preen and purr and crowd round them to compliment the child and clasp her to their bosoms. He never could make out what they said but it curdled his stomach every time. To this day he could not expunge the taste of his bile.

Nobody ever took notice of him; few even knew he was up there. Sooner or later the maid would find him and drag him back to his room again, this time carefully locking the door and pocketing the key. All these years later he still had that room, now entirely from his own choice. There were empty bedrooms on every floor, damp and decaying from years of disuse, but still he considered the attic his den and haven.

When they were gone, which was most of the time, the house retreated into itself and the crowd of liveried part-time servants dispersed to their other jobs. Only a skeleton staff remained while both his parents were on the road for sometimes as long as several months at a time. The reception rooms were no longer lit; the furniture was covered in dust sheets, while the brass and silver gradually lost its lustre. They lived upstairs on the top two floors with only a governess and a nursery maid to see to their daily needs and teach them their lessons.

They were both dead now, which was just as well. The images kept him awake at night but only when he remembered; he normally blocked them. He had hated them then, hated her still, yet was locked with her into a bond which there could be no breaking. This house, which had ruined all their lives, still shielded the secret that could not be told. He would go to his death before he ever revealed it.

*   *   *

Wilbur was right about the hotel. Their room was cramped, with an uninspiring view of the busy Cromwell Road traffic. The other guests were mainly tourists, American women in crimplene pants and uniformly white curly hair, like sheep. Mostly they only stayed a few nights, then another contingent would take their place. More Americans, Japanese; sometimes even Germans. Ellie, seated in the tiny lounge with her coffee and the morning paper, would watch their luggage trundling in and out. Lost without Wilbur barking orders, she wasn't quite sure what to do with herself now she was cut adrift. She'd completely surrendered her independence when she married him thirty-eight years ago, and although she knew money was hardly a problem, she wasn't sure how to access it. He had never allowed her a credit card of her own.

When she needed something, she had to ask; he kept tight control of the purse strings. He also insisted on keeping her passport; the only time it was ever in her hands was when they passed through immigration, after which she had to give it back. Wilbur put it down to prudence; Ellie was less sure. But here she was now, stranded in London, a sprawling city that scared her to death, separated, for the first time ever, from her over-uxorious jailer.

Harrods had virtually blown her mind, making her feel like an ant in an Eastern bazaar. So many people and so much stuff; she had wandered through ladies' fashions until her head spun. She treated herself to the luxury washroom, guilty at frittering an unnecessary pound on something that elsewhere in the store was free. But Wilbur had urged her to have a good time, so why not? She was surely worth it.

While looking for gifts to take home to the children, she found a quiet restaurant on an upper floor and paused for a sandwich and a cup of tea. She was all shopped out and had nowhere to go. She longed for someone to talk to.

'Will there be anything else?' asked the girl, hovering politely with the menu.

'A glass of white wine,' declared Ellie boldly, remembering that supper with Margaret. After which she would take a tour on an open-top bus.

16

Lucy Tucker was getting married. Her female colleagues at Lambeth Council were sending her off in style with a raucous hen night. After champagne with the boss in the office, they straggled in disorderly array along the riverside walk of the South Bank, after their ringleader, Dawn, who was walking with Lucy. Lucy, in her purple boho dress, was decked out in style in a bridal veil with a bouquet of lilies and roses in her arms. The rest of the group wore quivering antennae tipped with glittering silver balls. It was Tuesday evening and still very warm; she was taking off three days to prepare for the wedding.

They drifted along among the crowds, past the Festival Hall and National Theatre, towards the Oxo Tower where they had a reservation. All ten were well into party mood, Lucy's nuptials an ideal excuse for a rave-up. They lingered by each of the various living statues, passing comments, some of them lewd, forgetting in their fevered state that they could be overheard.

The one who all of them voted best was a shimmering Tutankhamen, as still as if he were really dead, his face concealed by a gilded mask, hands folded against his chest. The box he stood on was a cubic foot, the marvel being that he didn't even wobble.

'Wow,' said one of them. 'Look at that. See if you can get him to move.' Fall off his perch was what she meant. Dawn deftly flicked him a coin.

For a very long moment he didn't react then slowly, like an automaton, he bent at the waist in a perfect bow, hands still folded.

The girls all clapped. He was out of this world. 'Do it again,' they shrieked. How did he manage to stand so still for so long?

'Lucy,' said Gail, who had brought her camera, 'let's get a shot of you with the pharaoh. Go and cosy up to him and I'll chuck him another coin.'

Lucy, still draped in her wedding veil, minced up to him on her stacked-up shoes and coyly nestled her head against his chest.

'Kiss him!' they screamed and she turned to comply, but when she peered into his gilded mask the eyes behind it were fiercely alive and burned with malevolent hate.

She backed off like a scalded cat as a bolt of terror shot through her. 'I think it's time to move on,' was all she would say.

'What?' asked Dawn as they drifted away. But Lucy wouldn't explain.

The trendy restaurant, as always, was packed, with a celebratory ambience that completely restored Lucy's spirits. She was getting married. They checked her flowers into the cloakroom but not the huge box, done up in silver with ribbons and bells, that two of their number had valiantly lugged from the office. After they'd eaten and the dishes were cleared, more champagne was ordered. Which meant the speeches and the presentation of the microwave oven for which they had all chipped in.

'Thanks,' said Lucy, who couldn't cook. 'That's one of my problems solved.'

'So now we move on to the bedroom,' said Dawn. 'The gospel according to Jerry Hall.' A second package, this time bright red, revealed a sexy nightgown.

Three of them went to the cloakroom together and came back, after a lengthy pause, cracking up at some secret joke that it took them a while to divulge. They had seen this guy who was really neat, sitting alone at the end of the bar, film-star good-looking and dressed head to foot in black. They all craned to look but could not make him out; the area round the bar had really filled up. They amused themselves by laying bets as to which of their number would be the one to pull him.

'Not you, Lucy. You're disqualified.' The management requested they keep it down.

Sexy Leanne, the elected one, with her short tight skirt and incredible legs, glossed her lips and tousled her hair then wandered to the bar to check him out.

'Gone,' she reported on her return. No one there answering his description. Somehow, amid all their mitherings, he had managed to slip away.

Most of the group were catching buses. Dawn and Lucy and a couple of others walked together to the nearest station, Blackfriars. Lucy was heading for Monument to change at Bank for the Central Line which meant a long trek through a complex of tunnels to catch the last train home to Theydon Bois. They helped her with her packages and waved as she struggled on to the platform still decked in her bridal veil. It was well past midnight. There wasn't much time, and she still had to get through that maze of passages. Faintly squiffy from all she had drunk, with her wilting bouquet stuffed under one arm, she now regretted the stacked-up shoes and considered taking them off.

There were very few people around at that hour; the brightly lit complex was virtually deserted though she felt much safer down here than up on the street. The box was so heavy it weighed her down and, from time to time, she had to pause. Now she wished she had splurged on a taxi; she was getting married, for heaven's sake. She stuffed the nightgown into her bag and dragged the box along by its ribbons, accompanied by the irritating jingling of minuscule silver bells. As she hurried along the endless passages, she had the feeling she was not alone. She turned a couple of times to check but could see no one behind her. Only eight minutes; she doubted she'd make it. She ought to have asked him to pick her up. But that was no way to begin a marriage; she'd deliberately left her phone switched off. Start as you mean to go on, her mother had said.

At last she reached the escalator that led up to the Central Line. She balanced the flowers on top of the box and steadied it all with one hand. Still two minutes in hand; she might just make it.

There was movement behind her, she was positive now. She turned and a man had come into view, just setting foot on the escalator behind her. Lucy was gathering her things together – her handbag, the flowers and the cumbersome box – when the hem of her long boho dress got caught between two of the moving stairs. There was only a matter of yards still to go; she tugged at the fabric in panic. There were rapid footsteps behind her now; thank God, he was coming to help her.

'Thanks,' she said as she felt him close. 'All it needs is a mighty tug.'

His breath was warm on her cheek as he leaned towards her. It was only when the knife went in that Lucy realised how wrong she had been.

Her body was found by station cleaners a long time after her train had left. She was lying in a crumpled heap, the hem of her dress very badly torn, her presents and flowers strewn around her, the bridal veil soaked in her blood.

The cop who called next day at the town hall was older and handsome in a lived-in sort of way. The girls, still heavily traumatised, were summoned, one by one, to be interviewed. He walked, Dawn noticed, with a very slight limp but had intelligent eyes. He asked her to tell him exactly what had happened.

'She was fine when she left us,' said Dawn, alarmed and very much on the defensive. 'She got off the train at Monument.' The murder had occurred at Bank. The stations were part of a complex and interconnected.

'Had she been drinking?'

He had to be joking. A hen night? 'We all had,' she said. 'She was getting married on Saturday. We were giving her a send-off.'

'And she was wearing a bridal veil? And carrying a bouquet?' he asked.

He clearly didn't move in their circles. Where had he been all his life?

'Did anything you can think of happen that might have led

95

to her sudden death? Anyone else, outside your group, who might have been involved?'

Dawn shook her head. She had no idea. They were simply a group of colleagues from work who got together now and again for a drink or two and some laughs.

'She seemed very happy,' she added, somewhat lamely.

The cameras had managed to catch it this time, had recorded her struggling, first with the box and then with the hem of her skirt when it got snarled up. They were focused on her as she tried to free it, had caught the frustration on her face which turned to relief – and later terror – as she neared the escalator's end. The dark-clad figure who had followed her up at first appeared to be coming to her aid. Until he'd whipped out the bowie knife and moved so fast, all they got was a blurred impression. The technicians were working to try to sharpen the image.

'Were you aware of a stranger about?'

'No,' said Dawn. 'It was just us girls.' The guy the others had giggled about completely slipped her mind.

'Right,' said Brewster, checking his notes. 'That's all I need from you for now.' He still had another eight to get through, each as paralysed as the last, as well as the stricken bridegroom-to-be out in Essex.

'Let me know if you think of something. And, whatever you do, be careful.'

17

It was 8.51, the platform was packed and Dawn was still in a state of shock as she waited for her train at Aldgate station. What had happened to Lucy had left her reeling; the news had still not entirely sunk in though that stony-faced cop hadn't helped. He had spoken to each of the girls in turn, reducing a couple to desperate weeping. They had started the evening on such a high. It seemed that it must be the Circle Line killer who had now struck three times in less than two weeks. What had just been a newspaper item had now come gruesomely close to home. If only they hadn't left her alone with all that champagne inside her. Dawn shuddered to think that they all could have wound up dead.

It was 8.53. With luck, she would get to work in time for a natter. The rest of the group were feeling as shaky as she was. From the tunnel came a resounding explosion. Dawn was blown off her feet.

* * *

Ellie had made an early start. She still had so much to fit in. To think that Wilbur had really believed they could get to know London in a single week. The more she saw, the more she longed to stay on. She had loved going round on the open-top bus, which had shown her new areas to explore. Wilbur had seemed detached last night; irritated, even, that she was there. He was chatting to the man in the neighbouring bed; he made her feel she was intruding. So she'd only stayed a couple of minutes while she checked on his progress with the nurses. They reassured her that his hip was healing, and that he would be coming out within weeks. So, with a kiss and a girlish wave, Ellie left the hospital, feeling as though she had just been let out of school.

Monday had been Independence Day and she'd dutifully telephoned home, though she wasn't sure till the very last minute how much it was wise to reveal. Wilbur, she'd told them, had trouble with his knee and was having a medical check-up. They were all together at one daughter's house; she could hear the clatter of plates and everyone laughing.

'Is he all right, Mom?' They were screaming out greetings.

'Yes, dear,' she said. 'As soon as we get there, we'll send you a postcard from Paris.'

Today she was braving the British Museum which not been not included on Wilbur's schedule. But she wanted to see the Elgin Marbles; the story had always struck her as so romantic. Melina Mercouri. She remembered the fight and had also read Byron on the subject. She felt slight guilt at being out and about but, as Wilbur had said himself, there was little point moping around in that dreary hotel. Tom, the desk clerk, was not yet on duty but his stand-in told her the best route to take. Circle Line to King's Cross, he said, then change to the Piccadilly Line for just one station to Russell Square. She would not be able to miss the museum, which was vast.

At 8.57 she reached King's Cross. She was slightly early, but it didn't matter; she would take a leisurely stroll through Bloomsbury and look for the house where Virginia Woolf had lived. King's Cross station was in absolute chaos, with people screaming and rushing around and police making announcements over megaphones, imploring the crowd to stay calm.

'What on earth's going on?' she asked, grabbing the arm of a passing stranger whose face was bloody and clothes were all covered in soot.

'Bomb,' he said urgently, shaking her off. 'Terrible carnage underground. I'd move, if I were you, as fast as I could.'

So Ellie ran, not knowing where to, losing her handbag along the way and bumping into people in her panic. No one was interested in her; they were concentrating on getting out too for fear of another explosion underground. There was pandemonium everywhere, with sirens blaring and a huge police presence, many of them with sniffer dogs, some even carrying machine guns. It was a scene straight out of a World War Two film, with fleets of ambulances everywhere and bodies on stretchers with their faces covered up. Ellie ran as far as she could, until she was totally out of breath, then collapsed on a bench in a leafy square and wept.

9.17. Beth was running late but her staff would be there to open the shop. Though she usually tried to be first in, it was one of the perks of being boss. The train was packed, as it always was, and she glimpsed the wistful face of the beautiful stranger. How odd. If Beth was late, then she must be too. Perhaps at last they would finally speak. This train terminated at Edgware Road. She

would have to change platforms and switch to the City Line—
There was a colossal explosion and the train ground quickly to
a shuddering halt. The lights went out; they were left in total
darkness.

Beth could smell smoke in the putrid air. 'What's happened?'
somebody screamed. A man at the end of the carriage reported
seeing flames.

'Fire!' The word went round in a flash and people started
to panic. Some of the men took off their shoes and tried to
shatter the window glass; others were trying to lever open the
doors.

After ten minutes, which seemed eternal, the lights came
back on and there was an announcement. There had been an
incident at Edgware Road and everyone must stay calm. They
were going to evacuate the train as swiftly as they could. 'Leave
your baggage and stay in an orderly line.' They were told to be
careful walking on the track because of the live rail.

The beautiful woman, her face chalk-white, pushed her way
through and clutched Beth's arm. 'Please may I come with you,'
she begged. 'I think I'm about to have a panic attack.' She was
certainly shaking and sweating profusely and looked on the
verge of collapse.

Beth took her arm. 'Breathe deeply,' she said. 'It seems they've
got everything under control. Follow me and yell if you need
any help.' Thank God she was wearing trainers today, with a
pair of flip-flops stuffed into her bag. She looked at the other
woman's elegant shoes, obvious doubt on her face.

'Should I take them off?' The heels were high, hardly the
thing for negotiating a tunnel. 'Do you think there will be
another explosion? I'm feeling slightly wobbly.'

'Put your head down.' Beth tightened her grip and could feel her shaking like a frightened bird. 'We can only be a matter of yards from the station.'

Whatever it was must be very bad or they'd never have asked them to leave the train. The smell of burning was now intense; people were screaming in terror. And then Beth saw the west-bound train with the front all gone and the roof blown off. There were bodies and wreckage all over the track; she tried very hard not to look. This was more serious than she had thought. She dug in her bag for her mobile phone. She had to let her colleagues know where she was. She also wanted to contact Duncan and reassure him that she was safe.

Her phone was dead. She couldn't get a signal.

'The system must be blocked,' someone said. 'This looks very much like a terrorist attack.'

Part Two

Part Four

18

The bombings had come out of the blue with no advance intelligence warning. MI5 had received no message that al-Qaeda was planning an attack. The reverse, in fact; only four weeks earlier, the intelligence level had been reduced because the threat was judged to be at its lowest since 9/11. On the very morning of the bombs, in fact, the Metropolitan Police Commissioner had gone on air to boast that London was the envy of the policing world when it came to countering terrorism.

'I am absolutely positive,' he said, 'that our ability is there.' Though, on a graver note, he added that sooner or later an attack was bound to happen. Vigilance must be of prime importance. He implored the public to stay on the alert. There were ugly forces at work in the world which was now a restive and dangerous place. Britain was, after all, no longer an island.

In less than two hours four bombers had struck, timed to

go off simultaneously, three on the Tube and one on a bus, all in the central London morning rush hour. Fifty-six were killed and seven hundred injured, with the grim expectation that these numbers would rise. There were several theories about the catalyst, the most favoured being the G8 summit where the key world leaders were currently gathered in Scotland.

Brewster, however, with his specialist knowledge, had his own ideas about motivation. The day before, on 6 July, the capital had been in festive mood at the news that it was to host the Olympic Games. The television footage from Trafalgar Square showed Londoners celebrating in time-honoured fashion and could have been all that was required to spark off the suicide bombs.

There was likely to be a second attack; Brewster had seen the pattern before and London had always been an obvious target. The financial district, within the square mile, was where they were likely to focus their fire, the area where they could do the maximum damage. Despite the ring of steel that was in place, this time they might send in a car-bomb or, even worse, a loaded petrol tanker. Brewster would have liked to take command but his walking wounded status prevented that. Besides, they told him, he'd be far more use if, on this occasion, he stayed out of the line of fire and supervised the overall surveillance.

A car dropped him back at Meadow Road; Burgess should be there already. He had been on his feet since the early dawn, was at Aldgate almost as soon as the bomb went off and had been at Scotland Yard ever since, conferring with his bosses. His leg was hurting and so was his head. What he needed now was a handful of pills, washed down by a shot of single malt to help him endeavour to sleep.

* * *

One thing was sure, their assignment was suspended; the Circle Line was temporarily closed. The damage at Edgware Road and King's Cross would entail much heavy-duty engineering, before which they still had the delicate task of digging out the bodies. It was slow and disheartening excavation work, much of which had to be done by hand since even the tiniest scrap of evidence had to be carefully preserved. Brewster offered his services again but was rigorously overruled. His Iraq experience could be put to better use.

So it was back to a desk in Cannon Street until they had further information, knowing the odds were that al-Qaeda would probably strike again. His file on the Circle Line murder cases was relegated to his bottom drawer while a couple of uniformed cops took over the routine investigation.

It didn't stop Brewster thinking, though, as he lay in bed attempting to sleep. The gruesome murder of Lucy Tucker was the third he had half expected. Again the victim was a pretty young woman on her own, slightly drunk which would make her an easier target. The dark-clad assailant had seemed spare and fit as he came up behind her, offering help. She had looked relieved and spoken to him. She wouldn't have known what hit her.

Because of the timing of her death, it got submerged in the coverage of the bombs. Londoners now were on full alert, which was the only good thing about it. The killer should find it harder to strike again.

19

It took Beth a while to contact Duncan, the queues for the phones were so long. And when she got through, he hadn't heard about the bombs. He had strolled across the hill with his dogs and been in surgery ever since. They only summoned him to the phone because she was obviously crying.

'What on earth's the matter?' he asked in alarm, and when she told him he said he'd be straight over to collect her.

'Don't,' she said, getting a grip on herself. 'I only wanted to let you know I'm all right. It's like a battle station here.' She glanced round the hotel lobby, strewn with survivors with blackened faces, some of them with their clothes in shreds, all of them obviously shell-shocked. 'In any case, you'd never get through.' The sound of sirens was deafening. 'All I wanted was to tell you how much I love you.'

Celeste, nearby, was watching Beth but couldn't make out what she was saying. She could see, though, that she had now lost her cool and was in a highly emotional state. This was the woman who had helped save her life by taking her firmly into her care and leading her out of that hellhole of a tunnel. Beth wiped her eyes when she finished the call and gestured helplessly to Celeste. Then smiled and stumbled across and gave her a hug.

'I am sure things will be all right,' she said. 'I just needed to let my husband know. As soon as you're up to it, let's get out of here.'

Celeste, unaccustomed to physical contact, pulled back sharply and almost lost her balance. 'Thanks, but there's no need,' she replied rather stiffly. Then, more graciously: 'I don't know how I'd have managed if you hadn't been there.'

'Nonsense,' said Beth, 'though I must admit we came very close to being blown up.' She was quick enough to catch Celeste as she fell. 'Take your time,' she said to her calmly. 'I'm going nowhere till you're OK. And then you're coming home with me.'

Outside it was raining hard. The street was blocked by the emergency services and policemen were diverting all other traffic. They were going to have to fend for themselves but at least they were both still intact.

Ellie stopped crying and looked around. The square was eerily silent. A couple of pigeons came waddling up, obviously hoping for something to eat, but she had nothing to give them; her bag was gone. She had somehow lost it in her frenzied flight, too panicked to know what she was doing. There had been an explosion, the man had said, and there might be more to follow. He had told her to leave so that's what she'd done, too terrified to first get her bearings, and now she hadn't the faintest idea where she was. She also had no money at all, nor map, guidebook or travel card. She had even lost her umbrella and now it was raining. She could not even call for help since she didn't have a phone.

All around her were wailing sirens as police cars sped by with flashing lights but there wasn't a soul on the street apart from herself. So, since she had no idea where she was and her legs were still decidedly shaky, she decided the simplest thing to do was stay put. The rain had increased but she didn't care. Compared with what she had just been through, being soaked to the skin was the very least of her worries.

She was almost back to herself again when the air was split by the most colossal bang and a cloud of pigeons rose vertically from the trees. Another bomb and extremely near; this time there could be no doubt. Police in a passing car drew up and shouted at her to move away. It wasn't safe to stay where she was. There had been another bomb, was all they would say.

At last she encountered another pedestrian who told her a bus had blown up nearby. Round the corner from where she'd been sitting thirty people were reported dead. The transport system had been suspended. The only way to get home was walk, which was fine by Ellie since she had no money. The woman directed her to Oxford Street which was thronging with office workers doing the same.

When he finally surfaced, having slept in late, the streets were unusually deserted. For a second he wondered if it was Sunday but it wasn't. Though it had rained quite recently, the sun was bright and making the pavements steam. He slid on dark glasses and headed towards the station.

Terrorist bombs on the Tube, said the newsstands and now he saw that the station was closed. Sloane Square was virtually deserted except for the taxis. Since he had no means of discovering more, he decided to call it a day and go home. He would find out later, when she got back, details of what had occurred.

The fridge, always her preserve, was empty. Usually she shopped on a Thursday night. If he got hungry, he could get a sandwich from the Indian grocery round the corner. They were usually slightly stale but he had no choice. There wasn't a language problem there since they hardly spoke English anyway and paid no attention at all when he came in.

He drifted upstairs and, to his delight, found that for once her door wasn't locked. Which meant she must have left in a hurry; she was very seldom so careless. Though he had a duplicate key of his own, he preferred to keep that a secret from her. Knowledge was power; he had learnt that a long time ago. She had always been tidy, pathologically so, with everything neatly put away and all her bottles and jars lined up in straight rows. Tight-arsed cow. He fingered each one, unscrewing the lids to inspect the contents, occasionally spitting inside with malicious glee. She still used their mother's dressing-table set. He caressed the bristles of the silver brushes and held them against his face. They still had that faint sweet powdery smell he always associated with *her*.

He smoothed back his hair and studied his face, then massaged it gently with Crème de la Mer before perfecting his eyebrows with her tweezers. They might have been twins, people often said that, only he was ten years younger. He chose the foundation that suited him best and skilfully blended it into his skin, then fluffed it gently with her swansdown puff. A touch of colour just under each cheekbone and a thin line of kohl to enhance his eyes. His lashes hardly needed mascara but still he carefully applied it.

Pleased with what he saw in the glass, he turned his attention to her closets, running light fingers along the rails of expensive designer clothes. She was still the size she had been as a girl which meant that they fitted him too. He selected one of his favourites and slipped it on. Piled in boxes on the highest shelf were the hats their mother had famously worn. He stood on a chair and moved them all down to the bed. For twenty minutes he tried each one on, posing and flirting in front of the glass, until he was satisfied with the total effect. Then, making a sweeping theatrical bow, he blew kisses to an imagined audience. *Voilà – ladies and gentlemen – Esmée Morell!*

And then he laughed – oh, how he laughed – until fat tears rolled down his face, streaking the artfully applied maquillage and ruining the illusion. He ripped off the hat in a fit of hysterics and hurled it against the wall.

Ellie was flagging by the time she reached the park, glad at least to be wearing comfortable shoes. She crossed Park Lane by the underpass, then followed the signs to the Albert Memorial which was roughly in the right direction and ought to get her home. The rain had slackened and the sun was out. Away from the traffic, her spirits revived. The truth was she hardly missed Wilbur at all, had given him scarcely a thought since the bombs went off. Safe in his sanitised hospital ward, the odds were he wouldn't even know what had happened. He had his new pals and his poker games and a band of nurses to look after him. It amazed her how fast he'd become institutionalised.

Maybe she had been wrong all these years to give in quite

so easily and allow her husband to take control of her life. It took two to make a relationship work and, despite her silent rebellion, she wondered now if she might have been hard on him too. She had married so young, had not thought things through; had only in her later years begun to regret having not completed her degree. Yet who was to say she couldn't do it now? Talking to Margaret had opened her eyes to the possibilities that still remained outside marriage. If Wilbur could find other interests, so could she.

What she'd really lacked, since the children left, was a close and compatible female friend who shared her interests and sense of humour and didn't rely only on shopping and gossip. She found her neighbours trivial and dull, with their concentration on domestic things. Few had interests beyond their families and home. The women she knew in Chippewa Falls were fine for coffee mornings at the church but entirely lacking in intellectual challenge.

Margaret Gillespie had rejuvenated her, with her caustic humour and lively wit and droll way of looking at things, despite her underlying melancholy. Within just a few hours they had talked like old friends and discovered numerous interests in common. She had also been frank about her grief. Ellie suspected she might be lonely too. With a new resolve, she quickened her pace, determined to waste no more time. Like it or not (and she did, a lot) she and Wilbur were stuck in London, so should both make the best of it in their separate ways. She didn't begrudge her husband his poker: he had always gambled a bit on the side and at least, she'd joked, it was better than other women. It was not his fault things had turned out this way and if it made things easier for him, let it be.

She, however, had new aspirations and a brand-new friendship she wanted to pursue. As soon as she reached the hotel she would make that call. It was only then, with a sickening jolt, that Ellie remembered she had lost her bag with Margaret's phone number in it.

20

The reading group simply hadn't worked out. Margaret had found the other women vapid. It was not their fault; they were pleasant enough but largely tied down with toddlers and mortgages, few of them even as much as half her age. She'd enjoyed it at first since she'd badly needed a change of scene, something to get her away from the echoing silence. They had introduced her to Margaret Atwood and later to Zadie Smith. But mainly they discussed their problems, the potty training and sleepless nights, and Margaret had finished with all that long ago. Not even being a grandmother could revive her interest in baby care. Neither of her children lived near or included her in their daily lives. Except, of course, in the run-up to Christmas or when they were in need of a babysitter.

'Don't you carry your grandchildren's pictures?' The group were appalled by her nonchalance. To them it didn't seem natural that she appeared not to want to show them off. What sort of grandmother was she?

'No,' she said, not at all embarrassed. She hadn't even done it when her own kids were small. Too much flashing of baby pictures to her smacked of shallow boastfulness. Haven't I done well, was the implication.

She stuck it out for a couple of months, then made her excuses and left. She preferred to do her reading alone and not waste valuable time on trivia. Her mothering years were long since past. Now she faced a future on her own.

Card games had never been her thing so she also eschewed the bridge club. Haywards Heath was certainly socially rich. There were coffee mornings and bric-a-brac sales as well as tennis and bowls. After Jack's death she was swamped with invitations. But as the novelty of her loss wore off, so too did the telephone calls. If she chose to keep her own company, that was all right. She knew her neighbours thought her standoffish, which worried her not a bit. She'd had a long and successful marriage in which both partners had been well matched. She missed Jack's conversation most, and that could never be replaced.

So instead she threw herself into gardening, which had previously always been his domain, finding a new enthusiasm for it. They had lived there only a couple of years but the back-breaking work was already done. What remained was principally general upkeep, which she found unexpectedly soothing. She had started browsing through gardening books and swotting up on plants she didn't know.

'Blimey!' said Graham, her older son, when he caught her weeding on hands and knees. 'If the old man could only see you now, he'd be gobsmacked.'

She laughed. Fair game, she had left it to him in order to give him an engrossing hobby. She'd been pretty sure, had she tried to pitch in, that his own commitment might wane. He had faced retirement with gritted teeth, was not temperamentally suited to taking things easy. It had been up to her to provide him with targets: she had once even got him to ice a cake. As it happened, of course, it had not lasted long. At the age of sixty-two he had suddenly died.

Now, as Margaret mowed the lawn, she remembered Ellie Diefenbaker, whose husband had had that unfortunate fall which had interrupted their trip. She felt sudden guilt; it must be a week yet she'd still not got round to phoning to check how things were. Especially since those terrible bombs. Being right in the thick if it, with her husband stuck in a hospital bed, the American woman must have been petrified.

The meal they'd shared had been a real treat once Ellie was over the initial shock and the wine had eased her tension. They had found they had quite a lot in common, including a wry and subversive humour. If it weren't for the thousands of miles between them, they were surely destined to be friends. Though she hadn't taken to the husband at all, the type of boorish bully she tried to avoid. The antithesis of everything Jack had stood for. Time was passing alarmingly fast and, at this age, it was increasingly rare to find a new kindred spirit. As soon as she'd put the mower away, she would call the hotel to check up on Ellie and see if she'd like to get together again.

On the long trek back to Notting Hill, Beth attempted to get Celeste to talk. Now was the time to find out more about the mysterious stranger. To start with, they simply discussed the bombs, which looked like being a terrorist attack although, from what they had overheard, the authorities so far had no proof it was al-Qaeda.

'Do you suppose they'll attack again?' asked Celeste, still visibly shaken. 'I certainly won't be using the Tube again.'

'Don't let the bastards get to you,' said Beth, restored to her normal spirits. 'We can't allow them to frighten us or else their tactics will have worked.'

She had lived through some pretty hair-raising things but this was no time to be bringing them up. She'd been stalked by a psychopathic killer who had almost succeeded in finishing her off. To this day she had the dent in her skull to remind her.

She talked instead about safer things, the second marriage, the Marylebone shop, the daughter who was a dancer. 'She's in the chorus of *Anything Goes*. One of these days I'm hoping we'll see her on Broadway.'

Celeste had very little to say. Their conversation flagged. Inside she was churning with bitterness and regret. This confident woman seemed to have it all, even the talented daughter. There had been a time when her mother, too, had nursed such glittering hopes.

'I trained as an actress myself,' she said.

Beth wasn't surprised. With looks like that, given any acting ability at all, she would have been a natural. She waited politely to hear the rest but Celeste had relapsed into brooding silence. It was a good five minutes before she went on.

'I got into RADA. They said I had talent.' The statement appeared to embarrass her.

'What happened?' asked Beth, with genuine interest though not wishing to pry.

Celeste gave a brittle and humourless laugh. 'Life, I suppose you could say it was. Both my parents suddenly died and there wasn't enough money to cover my fees. I had to leave in my second year and get a job.'

Beth was appalled; what a terrible thing. 'Were there no grants at that time?' she asked.

'It wasn't that simple,' Celeste said grimly, regretting having brought it up. 'Let's just say that the legacy they left has entirely blighted my life.'

21

Burgess had really come into his own, working round the clock so that sometimes Brewster hardly saw him for days on end. Because of his specialist expertise, he had been seconded to the bomb squad, sifting through the debris from the recent carnage. He was highly proficient at what he did though few would have cared to have his job. He was always the first one on the scene, fearlessly leading the way down the burned-out tunnels. It was dangerous work and he was heroic, showing no sign of reluctance or fear. It was certainly nothing that Brewster would fancy doing. When Burgess came home, he reeked of smoke, combined with a more pervasive odour that took Brewster back, with a sense of distaste, to the scene of his own booby trap. There was no disguising the smell of death, which took much sluicing to get rid of.

Brewster spent most of his time at his desk, poring over the news reports or watching endless footage from hidden cameras.

Stuff about the bombers was emerging; all four were now proved dead. Suicide bombers, trained by al-Qaeda. He watched the coverage of their final journey, four British-born Muslims from the north, one of them deeply into his faith, two of them cricket mad. Casually dressed, they all had backpacks containing bombs preset to go off at precisely the same time. They also carried credit cards and other forms of identification, hoping to claim a spurious glory after their martyrdom.

Three of the bombs had exploded as planned, killing forty people as well as the bombers, and injuring over a hundred. The fourth man, apparently having screwed up, wandered for almost an hour through the streets before climbing aboard a bus and blowing it up. Witnesses spoke of his obvious agitation; too late he appeared to have changed his mind. Four young fools seeking paradise; it was hard for a Western mind to grasp such baffling motivation.

Life was brief and increasingly precious. The stronger he grew, the more Brewster acknowledged that. For a period after he'd been blown up, he had felt all incentive to live drain away, had lain for months in a hospital bed, indifferent to his fate. There wasn't a soul in the world left to mourn him. He would die, as he'd lived, all alone. But as his wounds began to heal, so did his spirit revive. Dead was bad; it was better to live. With each new day that resolution strengthened.

Random murder was mindless and cruel and didn't discriminate. Many among the bombers' victims had been of the Muslim faith. Risking his life, as Brewster had done, was designed to preserve democracy. There were times when a tyrant force, like Iraq, must not be allowed to prevail. Murdering civilians on the Tube was every bit as criminal. Terrorists had to be caught and stamped out before they could strike again.

But suicide bombers hunted in packs. The Circle Line killer was a solo act who had claimed three lives in less than two weeks, at intervals of a few days. In his way, he was even more lethal than those who at least had their crazy beliefs to support them. No one could tell when he'd strike again. Brewster decided to disinter the file.

He talked routinely to the girls again but not one of them came up with anything new. There was no dispute over facts or times on the night of Lucy's murder. He drove all the way out to Theydon Bois, to interview the shattered bridegroom, who he'd never really thought was a likely lead. The killer was almost certainly a stranger taking advantage of Lucy's inebriated state. She had made an exhibition of herself with her bridal veil and the silver box with its trail of tinkling bells. The station was almost deserted at the time, and its passages were very well lit; her progress was easy to follow on the closed-circuit television footage.

She had liked a laugh, the fiancé said, the nice young man with his stricken face, and always got on well with the crowd at work. She'd intended to keep on working, he added, at least until they started a family. At which his voice cracked and he couldn't say anything more.

22

Imogen was just out of the shower when Beth and Celeste walked in. The rain had finally stopped and the sky was bright.

'Mum!' shrieked Imogen, wild with worry. 'I heard the news from Julie. Thank God you're safe.'

Beth embraced her then turned to Celeste. 'My baby girl,' she explained.

Imogen laughed. She might look fourteen in her towelling robe with her hair dripping wet, but was in fact a grown-up twenty-two. Tall, like her mother, but finer-boned, she had a dancer's elegant posture. Celeste regretted having mentioned her own past, would like to take some of it back. She wasn't accustomed to talking to strangers though Beth, from the first, had made her feel like a friend.

Beth cleared her daughter's breakfast dishes and stacked them efficiently in the machine, then asked Celeste if she'd like a drink. She, for one, was gasping.

She carried a bottle of wine outside and pulled up a couple of garden chairs. 'Has Duncan rung?' she asked her daughter.

'Yes, and he's on his way home.'

Imogen went upstairs to dress and Beth raised a glass to Celeste. 'I think we can honestly say we deserve this. Is there anything urgent you ought to be doing, calls you might like to make?' she asked. 'I am sure my husband will drive you there if there's anywhere you should be.'

'No,' said Celeste. There was nothing that mattered. She had called the doctor from the hotel lobby and told him she wouldn't be in. Which was fine with him since all his patients had cancelled.

'Great,' said Beth. 'Then you'll stay for lunch.' She settled back in her chair to soak up the sun.

Duncan joined them, a rugged Australian with humorous eyes and a greying beard and the sort of handshake to make a woman feel fragile. He crushed Beth in a tight embrace and nuzzled his face in her neck. Although he tried to make light of it, it was clear he had been severely rattled.

'Thank God you're all right. I was worried,' he said and Celeste was pierced by a shaft of envy when she saw the love in his eyes. This woman certainly had it all: the kid, the house, the flourishing business and now this adoring man. Yet she must, at a guess, be pushing fifty and was nothing special in the looks department except for the glow she exuded from knowing she was loved.

Beth popped inside to knock up a meal while Duncan did the honours with the wine.

Julie hadn't even started out when news of the bombings came through. A colleague had rung to check that she was all right.

128

She was dying to get in there and hear things first hand but the man instructed her not to move. It wasn't safe; her presence wasn't essential. Julie instantly took offence; her job was every bit as vital as his. But her colleagues in Features were being sent home. The paper had ordered a fleet of black cabs since it wasn't safe to use the Tube, much of which wasn't running anyway.

'You can write about it from home,' he said, in an effort to pacify her. 'Why not go out and get some first-hand impressions?'

Julie brightened; a good idea. If she was quick, she could get in ahead of the *Mirror*. First, however, she made herself coffee and lit her first cigarette of the day, then settled down to watch the TV coverage. Within an hour of the bombs on the Tube, a number 30 bus exploded, killing a lot more people. Julie's enthusiasm rapidly waned; the vox pop interviews could wait. She would stick around here to see what happened next.

Meanwhile, she checked that Alice was safe and practically everyone else she could think of. Beneath her brassy exterior, Julie's heart was solid gold, though she wouldn't have cared to let anyone know that. Her call woke Imogen, who hadn't yet heard and immediately worried about her mother.

'I'd better get off the line,' said Julie. 'Call me when you know.'

Now was clearly not the time to ask Imogen if she had managed to dig up anything about the mysterious and fabled Esmée Morell. She got out her folder of notes, however, and mulled them over while she listened to the news.

Duncan kept the radio on to catch what was happening on the news and find out if there had been any more explosions. Imogen had to leave by five to get to the National Theatre on time. Duncan said he would drive her whenever she wanted.

'You're not going in?' said Beth, alarmed.

'I have to. The show must go on.'

'Surely not tonight,' said Beth. 'Who in the world will venture out? I wouldn't have thought it worth them opening at all.'

'That's not for me to decide,' said Imogen, born with the theatre in her blood. She had never missed a single performance so far.

Duncan offered Celeste a lift home. It wasn't out of his way, he said. 'Unless you'd rather stay on for supper. We can even find you a bed for the night if you're nervous of being alone.'

Celeste, unused to such kindness, was touched. 'Thanks, but I have to get back.' She still had the grocery shopping to do, had left the house empty of any supplies, though the news was now saying that most shops had closed early.

'Come again soon,' said Beth as they left. 'I am really glad to have got to know you at last.'

Chelsea was only a mile or so and the roads were surprisingly empty. People must be doing as Beth had said and staying home.

'I hope they'll come to the show,' wailed Imogen, hating the thought of an empty house.

'Don't worry,' said Duncan, 'I'll stick around and check things out before I leave. And I'll come back after it's over to pick you up.'

When they saw Celeste's house they were both impressed. It was huge and imposing, in Edwardian brick, with a handsome porch that added a touch of grandeur. All the curtains were partially drawn as though they had caught it napping.

'Crikey!' said Imogen, leaping out. 'Surely you don't live here alone.' It looked as large as a small hotel and must need considerable upkeep. She'd have liked to have had a look inside but Celeste was not forthcoming.

'More or less,' she said obliquely. 'I was born here.'

Duncan went round to open her door and Celeste emerged with the poise of a model, graciously allowing him to take her hand. He walked her across to the imposing porch and waited while she searched for her key. 'Are you sure you'll be OK?' he asked and she nodded.

'Unusual woman,' he said thoughtfully, heading now towards the river. 'Out of some bygone age. She seemed unreal.'

Imogen wasn't listening, though. She was staring back at an upstairs window where she could swear she had seen a curtain twitch. Celeste had implied she lived on her own yet somebody up there had been watching.

23

Margaret never did get round to phoning Ellie; her daughter-in-law, Amy, rang requesting a favour. They had Glyndebourne tickets for Saturday night, a work thing to which they should really go. She wondered if Margaret would come and take care of the children.

'Stay the night, of course,' she said in her abrupt, slightly grudging way.

Thanks, thought Margaret grimly, though didn't say it. Still, she hadn't seen them in quite a while and, away from their parents, the children were fine. Graham would come and collect her, said Amy, but Margaret preferred to be independent. She would drive herself over in the afternoon and take the kids out somewhere local for a treat. So there went the restful weekend in the garden she had planned.

Never mind, she mustn't be selfish; they were, after all, Jack's grandchildren too. Her crusty manner belied a generous heart.

She sincerely hoped that, when her grief was less raw, she'd be able to be a proper granny again. She forgot all about poor lonely Ellie stuck, for her sins, in that dreary hotel, wondering how to get to the hospital to beg the ghastly husband for a handout.

By Sunday things appeared back to normal, except that the Tube was still closed. We Are Not Afraid, the posters proclaimed, and Londoners came out in droves to emphasise that message to al-Qaeda. Chelsea was going about its business. The restaurants had all opened again and the King's Road shops were doing their usual brisk trade. Families out for a Sunday stroll dawdled along the riverbank or crossed the Albert Bridge to Battersea Park. It was impossible to cow the spirits of Londoners, many of whom had survived worse things than this.

In the house in Tite Street it was business as usual. Celeste was preparing the Sunday lunch. It was one tradition she insisted on maintaining. The only sounds in the cavernous rooms was the ponderous tick of the grandfather clock and the sizzle of sausages burning in the pan. She was slightly unsteady on her feet, having knocked back three sherries in quick succession as she vainly tried to mash the watery potatoes. The sprouts were already overcooked. Their sulphurous smell pervaded the whole of the house.

She had only learnt to cook by default since they could no longer afford the staff and neither cared very much about what they ate. For eighteen years they had lived this way, subsisting on an unvarying diet, abandoned by the hangers-on who had endlessly sponged off their parents. She did it all, since he offered no help, though only ever with deep resentment. Occasionally she would get out the Hoover but left the grandiose reception rooms to decay. There was no point, since they never entertained, in trying to maintain the splendour of their youth. Most of their time they spent apart, closeted separately behind closed doors in their different states of quiet desperation. What he did up there she had no idea, though she strained her ears to catch even the slightest movement. He was never up by the time she left and almost always out when she got home. They rarely sat down to eat together apart from this regular Sunday charade, a parody of normal family life.

Now, as she served the uninspiring meal, he stood there nursing a glass of claret with his customary blank stare.

What he wanted to know was what she'd been up to and who this man was who had driven her home. A big man, burly, with a greying beard, who had opened her door and helped her out then taken her arm protectively as he walked her across the street. He had watched them talking outside the house and had seen the way she'd looked up at him with a smile so luminous it knocked ten years off her age. He lost sight of them when they entered the porch but he had a graphic vision of him kissing her. The idea appalled him, almost made him want to throw up.

Minutes passed and the man reappeared, casually raising his hand in salute, returning to the car against which a pretty young girl was now leaning. His daughter, perhaps, with long dark hair and the lissom figure of a beauty queen. She was showing considerable interest in the house. It was years since he'd known her have any sort of boyfriend. Even the idea made his flesh crawl with rage. Although he detested her much of the time, she remained his only kin as well as his lifeline. His deepest fear, which he couldn't face up to, was that she would finally have had enough and walk out. He wouldn't be able to deal with that, would do whatever it took to prevent its happening.

He knew very little about her work, despite the fact he had followed her there several times. She kept that part of her life quite separate, rarely discussed it and never brought anyone home. He was jealous because she had somewhere to go, could hold down a job and earn money. He deeply resented still being dependent on her. He had lurked outside inconspicuously, a talent he'd polished to almost an art form, and watched a succession of people go in, mainly female.

So where had she suddenly found this man, with his sleek smart car and beautiful daughter who must be around his own age? Perhaps he had brought her to look at the house with a view to marrying and moving in. A ready-made family: there was certainly room. But what would they do about him? Now he wept and his tears were real. He would not allow it to happen.

He was in a mood, she could tell from his stillness and the mutinous stare as she served up the food. He was sick, she knew, of being a social recluse. This was not the way they had been brought up. Their childhood had been affluent and pampered, the house a magnificent work of art, its doors always open to the world. The world of the rich and famous, at least; the unclean masses were not included. Sir Edward Forrester and his lady did not know the meaning of democracy. They had always lived way beyond their means, in a manner they felt they owed their adoring public. The parties they gave had been legendary, the house the focal point of bohemian London.

They had shown off Celeste from the age of three. Dressed in a pretty party frock, she would be invited down to entertain the guests. She was used to being at the centre of things, knew how to smile and curtsey cutely, even sing a song when invited to. She had lived the life of a pampered princess with the whole of her life mapped out for her. With that name and those looks, there was no way she could fail.

Until the son and heir had arrived, which was when the public pageantry ceased. Since that single appearance at Drury Lane, Oberon Forrester had not been seen until his mother's funeral, eight years later.

She was in the kitchen, rinsing the plates, when she heard a great shattering of glass. She closed her eyes in apprehension; what now? He had hurled his wine glass against the mirror, the Venetian one that was worth so much. Part of her heritage too, she wanted to remind him.

Having made his point, he was smiling now. Don't tangle with me, was the message. Though unable to cope with the rest of the world, he always unerringly knew which buttons to press to upset his sister.

24

It was late on a Monday afternoon and Brewster and Burgess, for once off duty, sat in the stands at the Oval cricket ground, watching the England team warm up for the forthcoming Test Match series. Australia was fielding a formidable line-up but this year the British were optimistic, with Freddie Flintoff, their new white hope, in superlative form. It was long overdue that the Ashes came home, which today took precedence in Brewster's mind. What he cared about most was the team's maintaining its form. As the light diminished, they called it a day and the players trooped off the field. Brewster rose and stretched his legs, one still aching more than it should, automatically checking his phone for messages.

'Come on, old chap,' he said to Burgess, quietly snoozing at his side. 'Time to pack it in for the day. Tomorrow we're going to need all our wits about us.'

At which, on cue, his mobile rang: the duty officer at Cannon

Street. Brewster listened for a few terse moments. Then: 'Hold it right there,' he said. 'We're on our way.'

The woman who entered the interview room looked strained and haggard, as well she might. It was she who had found the latest body, sprawled backwards on a marble staircase, a surgical instrument dropped beside it in a spreading puddle of blood. It could be just a random killing but the sketchy details resounded in Brewster's brain. He nodded to the witness to sit, checked his recording device was on, made a note of the starting time then asked her for her details.

'Name?'

'Celeste Forrester.'

'Address?'

'Tite Street, Chelsea, SW3.'

'Age?'

'What business is that of yours?' she almost spat.

Brewster, surprised, glanced up at her and, for the first time, registered her looks. For a second he thought he might have seen her before. No matter what trauma she had just been through, there was no denying her flawless beauty or the great soulful eyes that instantly drew him in. Nor, he now noticed, the curve of disdain on her chiselled upper lip. He hesitated then left a blank. She was right; it was hardly relevant. He moved on.

'Occupation?'

'Receptionist. I work for a doctor in Wimpole Street.'

'Which was where the incident took place?'

'Correct.'

Even the memory made her cringe. For a moment she shuddered and closed her eyes, trying to blank it out.

He gave her time to compose herself while covertly stealing a closer look. Five foot four he would say, at a guess, with a perfect figure displayed at its best by the classically cut designer suit, set off by expensive pearls. Definitely class; he wondered why she'd be doing such a menial job. Fallen on hard times perhaps; no doubt a messy divorce.

He laid down his pen, leaned back in his chair and requested politely that she continue.

'No hurry,' he said. 'Please take your time. But tell me every detail you can remember.'

It was twenty to six but Celeste was still there, updating case notes the doctor needed for an early consultation the following day. She took no notice when the doorbell rang – Miranda worked until six o'clock – but when it rang again she pressed the buzzer. The doctor had already left, had a regular Monday-night session at the clinic. Celeste went on working and gave it no further thought.

After a while she paused to listen and, hearing no voices from below, decided she'd better check that all was in order.

'Hello,' she called from the first-floor landing. 'Is there anyone there?' When no one answered she went downstairs to look.

Which was when she discovered Miranda's body, sprawled backwards across the marble stairs, her throat neatly slit from ear to ear, the scalpel lying beside her. The blood was appalling, all over the stairs with splashes up the cream walls. She closed her eyes at the memory. What she recalled most vividly was the look of pure surprise on the dead woman's face.

'So what did you do?' Brewster asked.

'Screamed,' she said. And instantly called the police.

Celeste would never forget that scene, the mellow sunlight of early evening shafting between the heavy drapes to spotlight the corpse on the stairs. Miranda Perkins, who was fortyish, had worked in the practice for fifteen years. Not a friend but a long-time acquaintance, a woman of cheery disposition who chatted a lot on the phone. It made no sense, had happened so fast that the killer had slipped away without being seen.

They would have to look into the dead woman's life. Miss Forrester's too, thought Brewster.

She wasn't an easy woman to fathom, with her chilly façade and haughty eyes, though in her youth she must have been a knockout. Not that she wasn't quite ravishing now, with a timeless iconic beauty. Brewster found her hard to get out of his thoughts. As he went about his evening chores, grilling a steak while he watched the news then catching up on his paperwork to a Dizzy Gillespie CD, he ran through the interview over and over again. He went upstairs to the attic room he had set aside for his painting. He did his best thinking at this time of night with the phone switched off, a whisky beside him and a paintbrush in his hand.

The signs were all there, though did not yet add up, that this could be the work of the Circle Line killer. The viciousness of the knife attack, fuelled, he imagined, by uncontrolled rage, combined with the boldness of the choice of scene. Not the Underground, which was closed, but Wimpole Street in the middle of rush hour when shoppers and office workers were streaming home. To ring the bell and demand admittance displayed a level of reckless boldness that commanded Brewster's grudging respect. And to have left no trace behind except the victim. It had none of the signs of an accident waiting to happen. It must have been planned.

No trace apart from the murder weapon, wiped clean then left at the scene of the crime. An obvious choice in a houseful of plastic surgeons.

25

Celeste hadn't slept. She was far too stressed, her head in a constant state of turmoil. The world appeared to be crashing about her ears. First the bombs and those terrible scenes she knew would stay with her for the rest of her life and now the horrible murder of poor Miranda. The bombs had been bad but the blood was worse. She was stuck with a mental image she couldn't erase.

Dr Rousseau was kindness itself and suggested she might like to take time off while she came to terms with both traumas. 'You must not blame yourself, my dear, for being the one who opened the door. The crime rate in this city goes up every day.'

Celeste was startled. She felt no guilt, just utter revulsion at what she had seen and how close she had come, once again, to destruction. It had also brought back Sunday's events and her nasty little brother's ugly tantrum. The worst thing she could imagine now was to be cooped up in that hateful house with its shady and devastating history. Had she been able, she'd have sold it long ago and moved to something smaller and modern, where she could live in comfort on her own and make some semblance of having a normal life. But her parents had left it in trust for their son. Without his consent she was powerless to act and she couldn't afford to buy a place on her own.

Instead of a break, what she needed was to talk, to clear her head and get her perspective back. Cautiously, she telephoned Beth.

'I don't suppose you are free for lunch,' she said.

They met in a restaurant convenient for them both; quiet, discreet and not crowded. Beth, who was a regular there, had booked the best table in the window and waved when Celeste walked in.

'Good to see you.' She gave her a hug. 'How are you feeling now?' Celeste, she thought, looked pallid and very strained.

Celeste said she was over the bombs and filled Beth in on the murder instead. Beth was appalled; she'd read nothing about it in the papers. She listened in silence to the horrifying story, watching Celeste's composure crack.

'She wasn't exactly a friend,' she said. 'I didn't really know her that well. But we'd worked together for a number of years and to come across her like that on the stairs . . . ' Her eyes welled up with impromptu tears. Beth took hold of her hand. 'The worst part is, it was I who let him in. The murderer, I mean. Someone rang from downstairs so I pressed the buzzer.'

You could have been the victim, thought Beth but had the

sense not to say it. The scenario was quite grim enough as it was.

'So what happens now?' she asked Celeste. 'I assume the police have been on to you.'

'They have,' said Celeste, abruptly back on her guard. 'They hauled me in first thing this morning to answer the usual routine questions. There wasn't a lot I could tell them, though. Let's hope that's the end of the matter.'

She is holding something back, thought Beth, who was far too canny to probe. Sooner or later she would spill the beans, which was doubtless what this lunch was about. She indicated to the waitress that they were ready.

Julie's project had caught Imogen's fancy; she was suddenly keen to find out more. She loved a good whodunit and this was real. She had most of her mornings and afternoons free and nothing specific to fill the time before the evening performance. She had asked backstage at the National Theatre but not come up with anything much apart from one of the dressers remembering Esmée, though only just.

'I was hardly more than a kid at the time and she was a major star. I only remember how difficult she was.'

'In what way?'

'Oh, the usual,' said the woman, who must have been somewhere in her forties.

'Have you any idea what became of her?'

'She died at the height of her fame. It hit the headlines for twenty-four hours, something to do with a child, I believe, but after that she was yesterday's news. Typical of show business.'

'And her husband?'

'Sir Edward. He was really sweet, a damn sight nicer than she was. He died too, very shortly after. It was said, of a broken heart.'

'That's it?' said Julie, when Imogen told her, intrigued yet also disappointed. She had hoped the National Theatre might have yielded more.

'Have you thought about looking for their graves?' said Imogen. 'If they lived in London, they shouldn't be hard to find.'

Julie, the journalist, hadn't got that far. She resented Imogen's being so much on the ball yet had to agree it was a brilliant idea.

'Find the graves,' said Imogen sagely, 'and who knows where else it may lead.'

'What are you suggesting I do? Exhume them?' asked Julie sarcastically.

'The graves should give you the names of their next of kin.'

Julie pondered; she could be right. She could kick herself for not thinking of it first. Actors that famous must be listed somewhere.

'It's not the fact that they lived,' she said. 'It's how they came to die. Suddenly and before their time. Why was it all hushed up? Esmée Morell was right at her peak. She took the lead in *Follies* that year, which won a Best Musical award.' She had done her homework.

'Right,' said Imogen. 'I've nothing else to do. Let's get our spades and go and excavate.'

Lunch progressed and, as Beth had predicted, Celeste began to open up. She was visibly shaken by something, not only the murder.

'This cop,' she said, as she toyed with her food. 'Treated me

148

like a piece of shit. Barely gave me the time of day, just asked a lot of dumb questions.' Especially her age, which had really riled her, though she didn't exactly know why.

'What was he like?' Beth was hot on the scent, aware there were things Celeste still wasn't saying.

Celeste considered. 'He was rude,' she said. But had had the most disturbing eyes, steely and concentrated. At first he seemed not to notice her at all, certainly not as a woman. And that was something she wasn't used to; most men gave her a second glance, even now. 'He behaved as though I wasn't in the room, as if he was asking his questions into thin air.' He had scarcely even looked at her, the part that had hurt the most. He had damaged her pride; she would find it hard to forgive him.

He was tall and thickset with a rugged face and a scar, dissecting one cheek, that she found disconcerting. A man of action; she could tell by his handshake when he finally escorted her to the door. In addition he walked with a limp, though it didn't appear to impede his movements. A man who had known mortal combat. She found that sexy.

'What sort of age?'

Celeste considered. Mid to late forties she would guess. He had not been wearing a wedding ring though she'd kicked herself for noticing that, especially since he had made her feel so inconsequential.

'He acted as though I didn't exist, just another routine statistic wasting his time.' Celeste took a hefty gulp of wine. The pallor of her cheeks had gone; her eyes were now bright with anger.

'Well, he certainly made his mark,' said Beth, amused to be able to prove her theory. Celeste, aroused, revealed an astonishing beauty.

Celeste flushed slightly. 'It wasn't like that. But he almost made me believe he thought I had done it.'

'You!' said Beth. No wonder she was mad. 'How in the world could he justify that?'

'I was the only person in the house at the time, apart from poor Miranda. Plus I was the one who let the murderer in.'

'Come now,' said Beth. 'You're overreacting. Was he cute?' she added, with a knowing smile. There was more to this tirade than pure indignation.

'What, in my youth, we'd have called rough trade.' Celeste's expression was hard to read and she hadn't answered the question.

'So what happens next?'

'I haven't a clue. I just hope he'll leave me alone.'

26

Talking to Beth hadn't really helped. Celeste's emotions were all over the place. She couldn't stop thinking about the cop and his cool analytical eyes. It was a good ten years, at the very least, since a man had had such an effect on her. She didn't know whether to be mad or hurt, to cry or break his balls. Dr Rousseau, watching her shrewdly, was aware she seemed very much out of sorts. Miranda's death had clearly upset her profoundly. Since she refused to take time off, there wasn't a lot more he could do. He invited her out to dinner but she refused.

Dr Rousseau was a man about town, a Frenchman to the core. Though in his late sixties, he was well preserved and prided himself on his immaculate grooming. Whether he'd ever been married wasn't known but he squired many ladies to the opera and ballet and occupied a bachelor flat in nearby Devonshire Street. His photograph often appeared in the press, at fund-raising dinners or opening nights, and his list of patients read like Debrett or a first-class passenger list. Not, though, that he would ever divulge it. The keynote of his success was discretion. That and his skill with a knife.

Celeste intrigued him and always had, not only for her dazzling looks but also for her enigmatic reserve. She had worked for him for eleven years, yet he still knew almost nothing about her. He had seen her house, had once driven her home but not been invited inside. Though always polite, she shut him out, keeping him firmly at arm's length. No messing around with the staff was the implicit message. Which seemed a waste since both were single and she'd be a social adornment he'd like to flaunt. When he pressured her for information about the way she filled her time, she only ever gave him sketchy answers. Working hours were committed to him; she'd often accompany him to the clinic or even work a Saturday shift when justified by his caseload. Other than that, though, she kept to herself. He had tried, on numerous occasions, to woo her but was always met with tactful resistance. Which, to any red-blooded male, could only be a turn-on. One day, he was still determined, he'd win her trust.

Now, though, she sat at her desk and brooded; he couldn't manage to raise a smile. She went about her duties as though in a trance.

Beth conceded that Celeste was strange. A refugee from a time-warp. Yet something about her defensiveness touched her profoundly.

'I don't believe she has any friends,' she said to Duncan that night at dinner. 'She always looks so sad on the Tube and clung to me like a drowning rat the day the bombs went off.'

'You should see the size of her house,' said Duncan. 'I cannot believe she lives there alone and Imogen swore she saw a curtain twitch.'

'She probably keeps a mad aunt in the attic or else a Brazilian fancy man. With looks like hers, I can't believe that she hasn't a secret in her life.'

'Beautiful, yes, but not flesh and blood. A little too perfect to be mussed up. Give me a real woman every time.'

Beth laughed and dodged his lecherous swoop. 'Yet she's definitely hiding a secret,' she said. 'I think I'll ask her to lunch on Sunday, if that's OK with you.'

'She was only here a week ago and you saw her again today Surely the two of you don't have that much in common.'

'You'd be surprised,' said Beth with a wink. 'I have a feeling she may be lonely. I thought I might try introducing her to Richard.'

Duncan roared. 'Don't you ever give up? Besides, he's still got the hots for you.' Richard Brooke was a well-known painter whom Beth had known most of her adult life, had even helped finance at the start of his career. These days, however, he lived in France though kept his studio on the canal. Beth was endlessly trying to find him a wife.

'They wouldn't get along,' said Duncan. 'She's far too uptight for the likes of him. Can you imagine her in that filthy studio?'

'You never know. It takes all sorts. And maybe he'll want to paint her.' A nice little earner on the side that might open up new vistas for her. And possibly him; he had been on his own far too long.

'What is it about you,' asked Duncan, embracing her, 'that always wants to put people in pairs? You're worse than Noah. At least he was saving their lives.'

'It's because I am so happy myself, I want to spread it around,' said Beth, flinging her arms round his neck and kissing him long and hard.

'Break it up, you two,' said Imogen, drifting in from the garden. 'You are far too old to be messing around like that.'

Later, on the phone to Alice, she asked her to come on Sunday too. 'We could do with a bit of lightening up. My mum's inviting another of her strays, met in the bomb disaster, can you imagine?'

Beth's Sunday lunches were legendary, the hottest ticket in Notting Hill. A throwback to her catering days, she loved having people round her table. Since the shop took up most of her energy now, she tried to restrict entertaining to weekends. All were welcome, the more the merrier as far as she was concerned. If Celeste could come, she would build the guest list round her.

Beth's call helped to raise Celeste's battered morale; she still felt badly about the cop and the brutal way he had taken her through all those questions. What hurt the most was his studied indifference. He'd behaved as though she weren't female at all. Lunch on Sunday would make a nice change and get her out of the house. Oberon, for once in his life, would just have to learn to cope on his own. She would buy him something he could microwave and leave explicit instructions. It was time he learnt to fend for himself. He wasn't remotely a needy child any more.

She was sitting wondering what to wear and if she should

have her colour done when her phone rang and it was Brewster, the cop, saying he needed to talk to her again. He had further questions that wouldn't keep. He was sorry to disturb her.

'When?' she asked, inexplicably shaking.

'Tonight,' he said. 'What time do you knock off work?'

27

He caught his breath when she entered the room. She was even more ravishing in the flesh than in his tormented dreams. Cool, serene and immaculate, she scarcely glanced at him as he lumbered clumsily to his feet and offered her a chair. She was the kind of woman that, all his life, he had found distinctly intimidating: classy and aloof, way out of his league. He shuffled his papers while she settled herself, then, with an effort, regained control and began the interrogation.

How close had she been to Miranda Perkins?

Not close at all, said Celeste. They had been little more than acquaintances, with no real contact outside their work. Even there they did not do much more than pass the time of day.

So, no socialising outside hours?

None, said Celeste. She had told him that. With mild irritation, she watched him scribble a note.

What did she know of Miranda's life?

Virtually nothing, Celeste replied. Just that she lived beyond Baker Street. Wembley or Northwick Park, she thought. With her mother. She also knew that she sang in a choir.

Boyfriends?

How would I know? Celeste shrugged. Privately, she thought it unlikely but didn't want to be mean about the dead. Certainly not to this arrogant cop who seemed to be out to get her. Miranda had been nice enough, friendly, chatty, slightly over-weight. She spent a lot of time on the phone, gossiping with friends.

What friends?

There was no way Celeste could know that. Not only had they not been close, they hadn't even worked on the same floor.

Brewster paused and looked at her, his eyes, as before, expressionless, seemingly impervious to her charms. Not that Celeste could give a damn. He could tell she found him boorish and unappealing and couldn't wait for the interview to end. She was growing tetchy and tapping one elegant shoe against the other. Nice ankles, he thought, then looked away. He refused to allow her to get to him. He caught her surreptitious glance at the clock.

Not so fast, thought Brewster, hardening. She wasn't getting away like that. There was something about the frosty bitch that got right under his skin. He would keep her here as long as he damn well pleased.

'Did you ever have any kind of falling out?'

Her eyes grew wider; she was genuinely shocked. 'Of course not. I've told you, we hardly knew each other.' Miranda was older by several years and had been in the job that much longer.

They had lunched together a couple of times but found they had little in common.

'You came from different backgrounds,' said Brewster.

She looked at him with her chilliest stare, meeting his challenge head on. If he wanted answers, he must ask direct questions; he could not expect her to improvise. The intensity of his scrutiny was starting to unnerve her, though she'd die before she let him realise that.

'Tell me, Miss Forrester,' Brewster said, leaning forward with narrowed eyes. 'Who do you think might have wanted her dead? Or, for that matter, you?'

'Me?' said Celeste, caught completely off guard. 'Where on earth do I come in? I thought we were here to talk about Miranda.'

'You were the one who opened the door.' The only person around at the time.

He doesn't believe my story, she thought, suddenly chilled to the bone.

'Take your time.' He was on to something. Her eyes were wild and she kept on looking around. The more distressed, the more beautiful she became. He was right; she was covering up.

'I have nothing to add,' she said, suddenly hostile. 'I must go now. I'm late as it is.'

'Sit down,' he commanded as she started to rise. 'I'm not through with you yet.'

He stood up and perched on the edge of the desk, his eyes now slits of steel. 'Someone entered the house that night with murder on his mind, yet no one saw him come or go and he left no obvious traces. Miranda's throat was savagely slit yet you, just one floor up, heard nothing. No raised voices nor sounds of a struggle. Not even the click of the door as it closed. How do you explain that?'

Celeste stared back in startled silence. One of her eyes had begun to twitch. She looked like an animal at bay. He found himself unexpectedly moved which had not been on the agenda.

'Don't you find that strange?' he asked. 'That the murderer should have rung the bell at a time when everyone else had left and you weren't usually there. You let him in and she got killed. Mission accomplished – or was it really? Might it have been that he simply killed the wrong person?'

'What exactly are you trying to say?' She looked one degree off breaking point.

'Just,' said Brewster in a milder tone, 'that you had a narrow escape.'

He stood at the window and watched her leave, slightly thrown by his feelings. Part of him was sure she was hiding something yet another, perversely, was on her side. One thing he was convinced of, though, she would never willingly see him again. The consternation in her eyes had been sharpened by dislike. Before she left, he had handed her his card.

'Call me at any time,' he said, 'should anything else occur to you that might help.' Or, he almost added, if you need to talk.

There were things about this latest crime that didn't entirely match the others. Someone had taken a massive risk by ringing the bell and walking in at a time in the afternoon when the street must have still been swarming with people. At a time when the doctors could well have been there, not to mention some of their patients. Whoever it was would have certainly left prints, yet both doorknob and weapon had been wiped clean, which indicated that the killing had been premeditated.

Brewster doodled on his pad. What kind of person would act like that? A psychopath or an imbecile or someone desperately seeking attention. Unless, of course, that was not what had happened and the ice maiden was holding something back.

28

Tom helped her out when he came on duty by providing Ellie with a bus map. It was complicated but could be done; they leaned like conspirators on the desk and worked out the most direct route. He lent her money for a travel card, with a pound or two extra to cover her needs. She wouldn't have asked but had no other option. Wilbur had always kept her short of funds. She suspected it was to keep her from straying, another thing about him she didn't like. He might mean well but rarely showed it. Too often he'd publicly humiliated her. She took a book to read on the bus and a folding umbrella in case it rained. She headed first for Victoria station after which, according to Tom, the journey was easy.

Travelling by bus was a new experience though she'd liked the one with the open top. She was now too scared to go upstairs because of what happened in Tavistock Square. She loved the view from Westminster Bridge (Wordsworth had written an ode to it) though shook a little when she found herself facing the Eye.

Wilbur was absorbed in a poker game with three kindred spirits he had somehow drummed up without getting out of bed. He made it clear that she wasn't welcome, was interrupting the game. He had heard about the bombs, of course, yet remained unnaturally detached. His bones were fusing though he still wore the harness and had to use a bedpan. Ellie wanted a private talk; there were things she was not prepared to discuss in front of a group of old codgers she didn't even know. This was the longest apart they had been since their marriage.

Grudgingly Wilbur laid down his cards while she drew the curtains round the bed. Their conversation was stilted and dull. She tried to make light of her King's Cross ordeal but he only showed any real interest when she mentioned the loss of her bag. Then he blustered and called her a fool. It was just as well, he pointed out, that he'd never allowed her a credit card of her own.

Ellie responded with her customary mildness and requested funds to keep her afloat. The hotel bill he could settle himself but she needed cash for her daily expenses. He told her she'd have to get it herself; he had left their passports and traveller's cheques locked in the hotel safe. What cash he had he needed here for his now twice daily poker games. Everything else would go on his hospital bill. He was getting off lightly as it was since his treatment was covered by the NHS and all he would have to pay for was his bed. She wondered if he still intended to sue and, if so, who would be his target. British Airways, who owned the Eye, or perhaps the City of Westminster for having uneven pavements. But she knew enough not to go that way. It would only set him off again and that she could do without.

'Don't carry too much money,' he said. 'Since you can't be trusted not to lose it. And keep a detailed note of what you spend.'

It was her money too, though she didn't point that out. Her mind had already detached itself and was thinking of other things. Since they wouldn't now be going to Paris, she intended to spend to her heart's content. There were numerous shops that she longed to explore without an old Scrooge of a husband holding her back.

Once on the bus with her book on her lap, Ellie's spirits revived. The odds against being in another attack must be high. It was mid-July, she had nothing to do except see the sights and enjoy herself. She was even becoming expert at getting around. First she'd have tea at Fortnum & Mason, something she'd always wanted to do, after which she intended to look at clothes. Tomorrow there was the V&A where she could linger as long as she liked. And later she'd try another Kensington restaurant. She settled back to read her book and, when she turned to the place she had marked, discovered the slip of paper with Margaret's number. It hadn't after all been in her bag.

Celeste sounded agitated when she called, apologising for the interruption. She had seen the cop again and things weren't looking good. He had made her feel she was under suspicion, was scared he was going to arrest her.

'What?' said Beth, profoundly shaken. 'He has be out of his mind.' It was clear to anyone with a brain that Celeste was refined to her fingertips, apart from which she would not have the strength to slit anybody's throat. Beth remembered how frightened she'd been by the bombs, that she'd very nearly fainted. Sensitivity such as that could not, she was certain, mask a callous killer. 'Why on earth would he think that?'

'Circumstances,' replied Celeste. 'I was the only one on the scene at the time of Miranda's death.'

'And?' said Beth.

'And I buzzed him in. I ought to have gone downstairs to check. I just assumed she had stepped away from her desk.'

'Don't let the bastard bully you,' said Beth. 'Would you like me to talk to him?' She always stood up for the underdog, something her friends found endearing though occasionally intrusive. But Celeste was aware Beth's intervention might make matters worse. She had seen in the cop's reptilian eyes that he had it in for her big time.

'So what are you going to do?' asked Beth. 'Do you want to come over and stay with us?' In any case she'd be there for lunch on Sunday.

'I don't see how that would help,' said Celeste. 'If I disappear, it might only make matters worse.'

Beth thought about it and saw her point. But at least she need not face him alone. 'Would it help if I came too?' she asked.

Celeste, alone in her Wimpole Street office, found her eyes suddenly welling with tears. She wasn't accustomed to anyone giving a damn. But no, she said; it was out of the question. Though she'd turned to Beth in her moment of panic, she didn't want to take the risk of letting her into her life.

'That's kind,' she said, 'but I can't allow it. You have your family to worry about. I simply wanted to get it off my chest.'

'What do you think he'll do next?' asked Beth, aware of the customers waiting to be served, knowing she should hang up.

'I haven't any idea,' said Celeste. 'He seems to be playing at cat and mouse.' She was sure he got a kick out of jerking her strings. 'I suppose he will just keep his eye on me until they come up with another suspect.' The thought filled her with unspeakable dread. She hadn't really thought things through until now.

'Try not to worry,' said Beth consolingly, raising her eyebrows to one of her staff to let her know she'd be free at any minute. 'Once they've dug into Miranda's past, they're bound to come up with other leads. Who knows what murky secrets she may have been concealing.' Though, from what Celeste had told her of Miranda Perkins, it didn't seem awfully likely.

'Thanks for your support,' said Celeste. 'Promise you'll visit me in jail.' She tried to make a joke of it though wasn't very convincing. If they dug into Miranda's past they were likely to do the same to hers. The thought chilled her to the bone.

The doctor was showing a patient out and would soon be in to hand her the notes. She would have to go but Beth had helped calm her down.

'Are you all right?' Dr Rousseau noticed she seemed upset as she ended the telephone call. She was still chalk-white.

'Yes, fine,' she said, 'thank you. Would you like some coffee? It must be about that time.'

It was after five, and she was tidying her desk when the call came through she'd been dreading all day.

'Miss Forrester,' said Brewster benignly. 'I think I may have been too hard on you and that we should probably have another talk.'

She gripped the phone, too scared to speak, certain it was a trick.

'I am sorry to call so late,' he went on, 'but is there a chance you'd be free tomorrow for a drink? If you can't make that, perhaps some other time?'

'No,' Celeste said weakly. 'Tomorrow will be fine.'

29

As a birthday treat for her very best friend, Imogen got Alice a private box for a Saturday matinée of *Anything Goes*. As an afterthought, she asked Julie too, liking her more since their recent collaboration. Of course, they had both seen the show before, had been invited to the opening night and were at the party Gus Hardy threw for the daughter of whom he was so proud. But the show had been running for almost a year and Alice adored the music. She had even bought the cast recording which she played whenever she had the chance. Julie liked to make fun of her, though, in truth, enjoyed it too.

'It's over by five so come backstage and then we'll go out for an early supper.' Imogen had a rare night off; an understudy would cover for her. She hardly ever had time to socialise now.

Julie was pleased by the invitation, having always felt slightly excluded from their close friendship. Also she welcomed the chance of a snoop backstage. She didn't quite know what she hoped to find out but needed to get the atmosphere right to help make Rupert's TV presentation come alive. She also very much liked the idea of rubbing shoulders with the stars. The theatrical life appealed to her. She wished she had Imogen's talent.

The performance, as always, was a total sell-out and the audience roared and stamped their applause. The cast took five curtains which, for a matinée, was almost unprecedented.

Imogen, still wearing her soaking tights, had her hair tied back and was creaming her face.

'Be with you in a second,' she said, offering them both champagne.

Alice perched but Julie wandered, inhaling the evocative greasepaint smell. A handful of celebrity faces were crowded into the dressing room where two of the leading players were holding court. This was the life the Forresters had led, adulated by the crowd and mixing regularly with their peers in backstage settings like this. What had happened to cause them to drop out, right at the peak of their glittering careers, to such an extent that nobody knew where they'd gone?

Imogen was ready so Julie wandered back, more determined than ever to find out the truth.

It was another marvellous summer's night and the riverside walk was bustling with life. The world and his wife were having an evening out. The street entertainment was there in force, jugglers, acrobats, trapeze artists, even a jazz band playing under the trees. When London puts on a show, it does it in style. There was also Imogen's personal bugbear, living statues of all descriptions, posed every few yards along the public footpath. The girls stopped and stared at each one in turn, giving them marks out of ten for their costumes and the effectiveness of their silent performances. Some of them were very impressive indeed.

'I find them distinctly creepy,' said Imogen, 'though what they do is incredibly hard. To stand that still for hours on end is even more tiring than sentry duty. At least the guards don't have to pretend not to breathe.'

'Why,' asked Alice, who could be censorious, 'do they do it at all if they have so much talent? Why not go and get themselves proper jobs?'

Imogen laughed. 'They are resting actors and this just another performing art. Give them credit for dedication and having the guts to stick it out. I know that I, for one, couldn't possibly do it.'

'Also you must admit they are cute,' said Julie, who always had an eye for the boys. 'Look at the beauty of that face. Is it male or female? I confess I really can't tell.'

Beautiful, yes, but also weird. Imogen found the unwavering stare disconcerting.

They were all the same with their intrusive glances and the way they giggled among themselves. He hated them all, these vacuous women; what did they knew about art? They talked about him as though he weren't there and, despite the fact it was what he intended, their callous indifference made him mad, the more so since he could barely make out what they were saying. The tallest one, with the long dark hair, looked vaguely like someone he had seen before. Whoever she was, he would certainly know her again. The other one too, with the red spiky hair and a skirt so short he could almost see up it, laughing bawdily, not like a woman at all. She was over made-up and smoking in public as if it were socially accept-able, which it was not.

The women who'd raised him had not been like this, had taught him manners from an early age: not to whisper and certainly never to point. To treat other people with respect. But he had grown up in a different milieu, where manners were important and nobody swore and ladies were ladies, and acted accordingly instead of parading like half-dressed strumpets, showing the world all they'd got. The one he still lived with, whatever her faults, was always flawlessly coiffed and groomed with her elegant well-cut clothes and inherited pearls. She would never be been seen out dressed like that or make such a show of herself.

But, despite all this, they excited him too with their brazen laughter and come-hither eyes. They provoked a hunger that was new to him and which he found hard to control. Let them mock him then turn their backs. They would find he was not so easy to shake off. Before they knew it, they'd regret their rudeness and discover they'd bitten off more than they could chew.

Julie's project was steadily progressing. She had filled in the backgrounds of most of the stars on her list. She was getting nowhere with the Forresters, though, despite having trawled through the British Library website. In their time, both husband and wife had been celebrated. Julie found many reviews of their starring roles. She'd played everything from Titania to Medea progressing, as the years went by, to Dolly and Lady Macbeth. In her early fifties she had starred in Sondheim, earning the show a Best Musical award, after which she had completely dropped out of sight. Frustratingly, her bibliography said almost nothing about her personal life.

He had played Jimmy Porter and Hamlet, spanning the decades between the two with varying roles, because of his looks, as a foppish upper-class toff. They had acted together whenever they could and, at the peak of their fame, were rarely apart. They had mixed in celebrity social circles and their hospitality was legendary. At last she located their London address: Egremont House in Tite Street, Chelsea.

The first thing she did was check the phone book but nothing was listed for that address. Just thirteen Forresters spelt that way in the whole of Greater London. Julie pondered; she could try them all but would probably just make a fool of herself. They had both been dead for eighteen years and nothing was known of their children. Most likely they'd married and moved away and were living anonymous lives. But at least she now knew where to look, which was a start.

Celeste was preparing for her date with Brewster; he'd suggested they meet in the Royal Court bar. It was not very far from where she lived; he had chosen it for its convenience. It was years since she'd had any kind of date, if that's what this meeting was really about. She was not convinced it would not turn out to be a trap. She couldn't keep her heart from pounding or settle to anything for very long. She racked her brains and ransacked her closets for precisely the right thing to wear. Chic but casual was her style, especially on a hot summer's night. She owned up to finding him very attractive. She had to get it just right.

Having gambled on nobody's being at home (he was usually out on a Saturday night) she drifted around her room in her slip, sifting through armfuls of clothes. She checked them all out, on their padded hangers, arranged according to colour and season, and tossed a few of them on to the bed for donation to the local charity shop. She would not be seen dead in anything outmoded despite her lack of a social life. She loved the feel of couturier clothes, which she'd always taken for granted as her birthright.

In the end she settled for stark black silk with patent sandals to give it a lift. That with her pearls should do the trick, if only she knew what he was after. He had looked at her in a searching way and the steel in his eyes had seemed somehow softer. The fact they were meeting in a bar made her less apprehensive. She showered then carefully made herself up, resisting the lure of a shot of vodka. Tonight she certainly needed her wits about her.

30

So tonight was the night. They were meeting at seven. He was slightly surprised that she hadn't cancelled. He looked at himself in the bathroom mirror and fingered the prominent scar on his cheek. It was fading slowly, helped by his tan, but to him still looked very unsightly. He shaved with care, then splashed on cologne. For personal reasons which slightly confused him, he wanted to look his best. The evening was hot so he wore a blazer, teamed with grey pants and a plain white shirt. He decided to travel by public transport; the car might appear too official. He wasn't quite sure what his motives were apart from wanting to know her better. Something about her fragile beauty had started to touch him profoundly. Put at its basest, he recognised a damaged kindred spirit.

There was something enigmatic about her; underneath he was sure she was not what she seemed. She worked in a relatively menial job yet, he would bet, had been destined for better things. She'd been hostile when he'd questioned her, unwilling to answer even routine questions except in the barest of monosyllabic grunts. She had flared up when he had asked her age, though he now conceded that she had a point. He was totally out of touch with the fairer sex. They had started badly but perhaps tonight he could get things on to a more even keel. He had spent too much time cross-examining thugs. He needed a softer approach.

'Night,' he called out to Burgess as he left. Usually they spent the weekends together but on this occasion he preferred to operate alone.

He deliberately got there ahead of time and ordered a double Scotch. He positioned himself at one end of the bar to be instantly visible when she arrived. He wondered now if he'd done the right thing, expecting a woman of class like her to enter this place on her own. But at least he had come all the way to Chelsea. He reminded himself that it wasn't a date; they still had unfinished business that needed unravelling.

Celeste was a studied ten minutes late, though the walk could have taken only half that time. He rose to his feet and politely extended his hand. He wanted to tell her how great she looked but wasn't sure it would go down well. Instead he simply asked what she'd like to drink. She chose white wine and he topped up his Scotch, then led her over to a quiet table. He saw the way men looked at her. Up close she was even more stunning than he had remembered.

'How are you?' he asked, once they were settled. 'Are you coming to terms with what happened?'

'As much as I can. I still can't sleep. But at least the image of Miranda's face no longer haunts me at night. Though, I confess,

I still feel terribly guilty.' She sipped her wine, clearly ill at ease, fiddling nervously with her pearls. Now they were face to face again the situation felt awkward.

Brewster switched to another tack. 'Tell me about yourself,' he said. 'Where you come from, that sort of thing. The kind of childhood you had.'

She looked up, startled, caught unawares. For a second he thought she might even walk out. A wash of colour highlighted her delicate cheekbones.

'Why should you want to know about me? It's Miranda, surely, we are here to discuss. I can't see where I fit into the picture.'

'You were the last one to see her alive. And you worked with her for a number of years. As you yourself said, it was you who opened the door.'

For a moment Celeste stared into her glass, then raised her great luminous eyes to his. 'I have told you all I know,' she said. 'Please believe me.'

He wanted to do so but sensed that she lied. Though to what degree, he was still unsure. Again he noted that one of her eyes was twitching.

He refrained from lighting a cigarette though he always thought better when he smoked. 'Let's imagine,' he said, leaning back, 'that Miranda was not the intended victim. That who-ever it was who slit her throat, by accident got the wrong person.'

Now she was pale and avoiding his gaze. He knew for certain she was holding something back.

'Why do you work for a plastic surgeon? You're not the recep-tionist type.'

'It pays the bills,' she said with a shrug. 'I wasn't trained to do anything else and have no one else to support me.'

'Divorced?' he asked, risking her wrath, and watched her jaw tighten slightly.

'No,' she said. 'I was never married.' *Not that it's anything to do with you.* 'I really can't see where these questions are leading.' *Cut to the chase,* she implied.

'Answer them, please. Where did you grow up and what sort of school did you go to?'

'My family has always lived in Chelsea. I was privately tutored at home.'

He'd been right about the pedigree, then. She was bona fide top drawer. The haughty manner and poise were indeed inbred.

'What was it that your father did?' *Undoubtedly he had been self-employed. Probably didn't work at all if you took account of the daughter.*

She was so long answering that Brewster wondered what she might be concealing. He was in no hurry and relaxed with his drink. He liked the ambience of the bar. This meeting was out of working hours; he had all the time in the world.

At last she looked him straight in the eye. 'Both my parents were on the stage. Edward Forrester and Esmée Morell. In their time they were quite well known.'

If she'd hoped to impress him, it hadn't worked. Neither name meant anything to him.

'Still alive?'

'No, both dead for years. Nothing interesting there, I'm afraid. Thank you for the drink. I must go. I hope I've not wasted your time.'

He had touched a nerve. It was time to quit. He dropped his card on the bill. He knew precisely when to back off, when the suspect was showing sudden signs of panic. He would do his research then bring her back in to answer further questions.

They stepped out into the busy street and Brewster offered to get her a cab but Celeste said she'd rather walk, it was very near. Despite her protests, he insisted on escorting her home. On the corner of Tite Street she held out her hand.

'There's no need to come any further,' she said. 'I'm just down there, half a block away. Here is the best spot for you to get a taxi.'

He tried to argue but she turned away, unexpectedly chilly and withdrawn. Whatever it was she was covering up obviously meant a lot. He watched her as she walked away, calm and in total control of herself, without a backward glance. She didn't even turn when she reached her house, just paused in the porch while she found her key, closing the door in his face. He heard the click. Brewster, reluctant to call it a night and now even more intrigued by Celeste, advanced discreetly on the other side of the street. There was something about her, he wasn't sure what, that had caught him in a vulnerable spot so that now he had an urgent desire to get to know her better. Not just as a murder suspect; privately, as a woman.

He stayed in the shadows, impressed by her home which was grander than he had ever imagined, especially for a receptionist living alone. He watched her progress through the house as she turned on lights and then switched them off, until she appeared at a second-floor window, pulling the curtains shut. The show was over yet still he lingered, lighting another cigarette. He found it hard to tear himself away.

Right at the top, in what must be the attic, a gentle flickering light appeared. A light so pale it was probably a candle, wavering in front of the window. Not strong enough to show anything much except the dark outline of a motionless figure. He stayed there, watching, until the light went out.

31

A lice couldn't make it after all; her parents expected her home. But, even so, Beth had ten for lunch that Sunday. She cooked a dish of succulent pork that positively melted in the mouth, garnished with roast potatoes and baby parsnips. Duncan had chosen a fine Bordeaux that enhanced the delicacy of the roast. To start with, Beth had made them artichoke soup.

Celeste, at first, felt the odd one out since everyone else seemed to know each other but they all made an effort to make her feel at home. Duncan greeted her like an old friend and asked, with real concern, how she was feeling.

'Much better,' she said but did not expand, could not explain how her outlook had subtly altered. She badly needed to talk to Beth and catch her up on last night's encounter which had turned out not to be the date she'd expected. He'd been very affable and looked good in plainclothes, yet in the end all it turned out to be was a slightly veiled attempt at further interrogation. Apart from that, she was looking great. Despite the fact she had hardly slept, her eyes were bright and her skin translucent, a transformation from how she had looked the first time Duncan had met her. A striking woman, he now conceded, slightly less weird than he had previously thought.

Beth and Duncan seemed ideally matched, warm and generous hosts. From the frequent looks she saw them exchange, it was clear they were still very much in love. Celeste, unusually, found herself empathising. It wasn't a feeling she had known first hand, not even in her tempestuous youth when scalps came two a penny and she'd scorned them all. Then men had been mere commodities, to be used, discarded and instantly forgotten. In her heyday she had broken numerous hearts. Today, however, she felt oddly chastened; still not clear about how things had gone last night.

Richard Brooke, an eminent painter, was seated next to Celeste at lunch and she sensed, from the rapt attention he paid her, that she hadn't entirely lost it. Two men in less than twenty-four hours. Her old self wouldn't have even noticed but Beth, aware of her slight agitation, assumed that Richard had scored.

Later, however, in the kitchen where she followed Beth to offer a hand, Celeste was almost bursting to unload.

'I saw him again last night,' she said 'He took me out for a drink. Though it wasn't so much a date as an interrogation.'

Beth was startled. 'The cop, you mean?' Could it be the relationship was hotting up? Surely he couldn't really think Celeste was a killer?

'He asked me loads of personal questions quite unconnected

with Miranda's death. I seriously think he has me down as a suspect.' She didn't add that she fancied him, had found his aggressive male presence attractive. Had wished it had been a genuine date that might have turned into more.

'How did he leave things?'

'In the air. Though I have no doubt I'll be hearing from him again.'

It was early evening when she wandered home, and the bells of St Luke's were ringing. She felt like a stupid schoolgirl, all het up. For a few brief hours she had sensed romance, had indulged herself in the impossible dream, when all the time he'd been trying to trap her into giving herself away. *He thinks I did it, killed Miranda.* The enormity of the realisation almost stopped her in her tracks. He had sensed she was attracted to him and used it as a weapon against her. By delving into her secret past, he was finally showing his hand. She was suddenly scared; he was a very tough man who would stop at nothing to track down a killer. He had worked in war zones; she knew that from his scars.

She was sick of continually carrying the can for what had happened all those years ago. Her career, her marriage prospects, her life had all been sacrificed to the one end, covering up and protecting the family honour. They were decently buried and forgotten while she still hid in that terrible house, having to keep herself to herself and her profile as low as she could, in constant fear of the knock on the door she was scared would one day come.

As she entered the house, she knew he was home though nothing except the clock's steady ticking disturbed the somnolent silence. She hadn't lived with him all these years without being able to sense his malevolent presence. She still took care of his basic needs, as she had for most of his life. But now he was grown with a life of his own, though she knew very little about it. He remained her personal albatross, hung like a boulder round her neck. Whenever happiness threatened to strike, he always contrived to destroy it.

She had no idea how he spent his time; when she left for work he was still asleep and when she came home he was gone. The only time they sat down together was for Sunday lunch, as they always had, but which today she had left him to eat on his own. It had been ready for him on a plate in the fridge with clear instructions as to how to heat it. When she checked, the plate was in the sink, along with the crystal goblet he had used. He never lifted a finger to help, something she'd given up worrying about, the result of being first spoilt and later neglected.

Used to it, though, after all these years, she dropped her handbag and wrap on a chair while she tidied the kitchen and carefully rinsed the glass he should not have been using. All they had left was this dwindling inheritance. They'd already been forced to sell some of the pictures. Once it was gone, she didn't know how they would cope.

When he rose at noon and found her not there, he flew into a terrible rage. Sunday lunch was their special time which, throughout their lives, had been a kind of ritual. She had left a note saying she'd gone out for lunch and telling him how to heat the cottage pie. She had set the dining-room table for one, with a damask napkin and a rose in a glass, and the sherry bottle on its silver coaster.

To hell with that. He hated sherry. Why did she treat him

like a child? He went down to the cellar again, to plunder more of his father's claret, then selected an eighteenth-century glass goblet from which to swig it down. He liked the finer things in life; it was, after all, how he had been brought up. As he sat at the table in the cavernous room, with the sunlight streaking through the heavy curtains, he studied the rose and uncomfortable memories began to filter through from his subconscious. The house had always been filled with flowers, one of his mother's particular foibles. She had made a personal statement out of arranging them herself. His mind clicked back to those opulent days when the house had been at its glorious best as, indeed, had his very gregarious mother. Celeste was a pale imitation of her and had cut their excesses after she died. He resented that and the way that she kept him imprisoned.

Recently she had been going out more; he had glimpsed her with that man and his beautiful daughter. She had only said that he was a friend but she had no friends, as far as he knew. Certainly none he'd ever met. The house was impressive and surely a bait for any loner with marriage in mind. She was long past her best but even he could see she still retained some of her charms. He would not allow her to marginalise him by bring strangers into their closeted life. His fingers tightened round the stem of the glass. He would sooner break her first.

He had killed the woman just to show who was boss, slitting her throat from ear to ear. The thrill he'd derived from watching her bleed was better than any of the ones before. He had simply dispatched the others in a hurry. This one he had watched die. He had not expected there to be so much blood. Slicing through the jugular had produced a fine spray which soaked his T-shirt and matted his glossy black hair. He would use the lavatory close to the station to clean himself up and change his clothes. He always carried his leather bag, containing the tricks of his trade.

She had needed that lesson to bring her to heel, to remind her what he was capable of. And yet she was out, for the first time ever, leaving him to eat alone on a Sunday.

Last night he had waited until she came in, had stood at the window and seen the guy, skulking like a fugitive in the shadows. He was slightly shorter than the one before, had not had the telltale beard, yet had stuck around for at least ten minutes, lighting one cigarette from another, like a lovelorn schoolboy after a bitch on heat. He would not allow her to act this way; it was not the way she'd been raised. If the lesson he'd taught her was not enough, he would show her the full extent of his rage. She must not even think about walking out.

He wolfed down the pie which she'd bought from Marks and followed it with cheese from the fridge. Then finished the bottle and went upstairs to wreak a little more havoc.

When she saw the damage he had done to her room, she almost abandoned him then and there. Her drawers were all open, their contents displayed, as though a burglar had been through them all, taking nothing but mutilating all he could. Her perfume bottles had been thrown at the wall so the place smelt like a brothel and the expensive lotions and creams she used had been smashed and ground into her Persian rug, another legacy from her mother's boudoir.

Her clothes had been casually strewn on the floor and some were ripped where he'd tried them on in too much excitement to treat them with proper care. The hats were scattered all over the room. She wept profusely as she gathered them up and tried ineffectively to repair the damage.

He was out of control. She'd not seen him this bad. She had no idea what had brought it on but a terrible thought she had tried to suppress no longer seemed quite so far-fetched.

32

Margaret was delighted when Ellie rang, as well as very contrite. She had meant to be in touch, she said, but circumstances had intervened. She hoped the news of Wilbur was better and that he would soon be out.

'Perhaps we can get together again before you return to the States,' she said.

'That's precisely why I'm calling,' said Ellie. 'I want to invite you to lunch.'

Since she still hadn't seen the Elgin Marbles, they arranged to meet at the British Museum where she had heard the restaurant was very good. She said she would book a table for Thursday. Wilbur was being discharged the following day.

Ellie was managing well on her own, with the help of Tom and her travel card, but lacked a congenial companion to do things with. Margaret was right on her wavelength, she felt; she'd enjoyed her conversation and quirky humour.

Money had ceased to be a problem since she'd got her hands on the traveller's cheques. She could replicate her husband's signature well enough to fool a cashier. She had also liberated her passport and the travel tickets that Tom had exchanged. It did seem a terrible waste not to use them but as soon as Wilbur was back on his feet he planned to fly straight home.

Julie had a dental appointment, her regular check-up in Markham Street, so since she would be in the neighbourhood it made sense to look for Egremont House. None of her colleagues would notice her absence; they'd all be glued to the opening of the First Test. Her teeth were perfect, which was no surprise, so she got out after a scrape and polish and zigzagged towards the river in search of Tite Street. It wasn't far. She was there in five minutes and strolled the few blocks down from Tedworth Square, checking out every house. Some had numbers but this one did not, at least from the details on the Internet. She saw a blue plaque for Oscar Wilde and another, nearby, for James Whistler but nothing for either Esmée Morell or her husband Edward Forrester. It was blazing hot and good to be out; better than being stuck in that air-conditioned building. If anyone checked she would say she'd been doing research.

She got to Dilke Street and found the sketch-club then stopped an old man and politely asked if he'd heard of Egremont House. Indeed he had; he lived in the street. They were standing almost outside it. He pointed towards an imposing building in Edwardian brick with an ornate porch that Julie had mistaken for a hotel.

'Do you know if anyone lives there?' she asked, not quite believing her luck. 'Indeed,' said the man, 'though it looks deserted, I occasionally see people coming and going.'

'But you don't know their names?'

'I do not,' he said. 'But a young man is sometimes there at this time of day.' He checked his watch; it was half past two. He was on his way to buy a paper.

Julie thanked him then, drawing a deep breath, walked up to the big front door and boldly rang the bell.

Lunch at the British Museum was great, the restaurant a triumph. Their table looked over the central courtyard and the menu was unusual and eclectic. Ellie asked Margaret to choose the wine; Wilbur didn't like her to drink, found it unbecoming in a woman. But now she was out from under his thumb, she intended to do as she darned well pleased. It was good to have found a kindred spirit in London.

Margaret asked how Wilbur was though, in truth, she couldn't care less. The little she'd seen of the grumpy old boor did not incline her to improve on the acquaintance. She already had the impression from Ellie that he must be a bit of a trial to live with.

'Cantankerous,' said Ellie frankly. 'Though he's taken it all surprisingly well.' She told her about his band of cronies and their peripatetic poker game, at present focused round Wilbur's bed since he was unable to move. 'It's exactly like a men's club,' she said. 'Without the brandy and cigars.'

Margaret laughed. She could well imagine, though Jack had not been remotely like that, having always rather preferred the company of women. She told Ellie a bit about life in Croydon and how they'd moved further out when he retired.

'I like the house but it's lonely,' she said. She hadn't expected him to die.

They talked a little about their children and Margaret pulled a slight face. Two boys, she said, with ambitious wives with neither of whom she saw eye to eye. 'I think they consider me slightly past it. Except, of course, when they need a babysitter.'

Ellie laughed. Her thoughts entirely; both her daughters were much the same. 'They think they're all so modern and with it, despise the mothers like you and me who had no option but to stay at home and give them so much of our time.'

The wine was a Chilean Chardonnay which went very well with the seared-tuna salad. Ellie commended Margaret on her choice.

They moved on comfortably to other things, including their mutual love of books. They shared, it emerged, several favourite authors, obviously liked the same things. Margaret told her about the reading group and what a non-starter that had been. Ellie talked about life in Chippewa Falls.

'At least you're not far from London,' she said. 'Imagine living, as I do, out in the sticks.'

Their conversation flowed so freely, they were both amazed when they saw the time. Margaret had a train to catch and Ellie must make her nightly visit to Wilbur.

'Now that he's almost better,' she said, 'he is back to being a grump again. Though he's bonded in a major way with those other pathetic old fools.'

Margaret laughed at Ellie's directness. She certainly pulled no punches. She regretted that they lived such a distance apart. Ellie mentioned the Paris trip, now sadly consigned to the rubbish bin. 'As soon as Wilbur can walk,' she said, 'he insists on going straight home.'

'Well, please stay in touch and come back soon.' Margaret realised, to her surprise, how much she was going to miss her amusing new friend. 'And next time you're over, you must come to Haywards Heath. It's hardly swinging but does have its own rustic charm.'

They hugged and went their separate ways. It was only at Victoria station that Margaret discovered there had been more bombs which had luckily failed to go off.

He was checking the weather before going out when his eye was caught by two people outside, talking in the street. An elderly gent he knew vaguely by sight in conversation with a girl in a very short skirt. She was waving a piece of paper around and glancing at all the houses. To his consternation, the old gent turned and pointed straight at where he was standing. He was saying something and she was nodding, then he turned and shuffled away. At which point, to his absolute horror, she stepped into his porch.

He skipped out of sight with a quickening pulse and flattened himself against the wall, as if she could see him up here on the attic floor. Something about her seemed vaguely familiar; he had seen that spiky red hair before as well as the skirt that could hardly be classed as decent. His heart beat faster and his hands were clammy. He could not imagine what she wanted with him or what that nosy old bastard could possibly have said.

He went downstairs very cautiously in case she peered through the letter box. She looked the sort who would stick her nose where it definitely wasn't wanted. Then it clicked where he'd seen her before: Saturday night near the National Theatre. She had wandered by with two other girls, one of whom he'd seen hanging around this house. The tall one with the long dark hair had been in the car that brought Celeste home. The daughter of the bearded man he suspected was a suitor.

He could see her outlined against the glass as she stood there, waiting for someone to answer. For all he cared, she could stand there all day, though it stopped him going out. He moved with stealth into the kitchen and waited for her to leave.

He was suddenly gripped by colossal rage; they should mind their own business and leave him alone. They were vermin, every last one of them, and needed to be wiped out.

33

Tamara, Lady Fermoy-French came bowling out of Daphne's late, after a very long lunch with her three dearest friends. Dottie, Annabel and Plum were up from the shires on a shopping spree, culminating in their annual reunion at one of the hottest watering-places in town. Tamara was wearing a Pucci two-piece and was slightly unsteady on her feet. Tonight was cocktails with the Peruvian ambassador. She ought to be home at the latest by six in order to get dolled up. But first she had a gift to buy; her husband's niece was getting married and had her list at Peter Jones (the china department, of course).

The afternoon was bright and hot; the streets were alive with shoppers. She tripped along on her Manolo Blahniks, oblivious of the covetous stares at her heavily manicured and bejewelled hands. Her husband, Peregrine, scolded her for flaunting his wealth quite so blatantly but what was the point of having it at all if you kept it locked up in the safe? Though no longer in the first flush of youth, she desperately tried to fend off age with strenuous exercise regimes as well as the surgeon's knife. Not a nice woman; Lady Fermoy-French had an ungenerous heart.

At Peter Jones she scanned the list, silently sneering at some of the choices. So many of the young these days possessed no concept of style. Still, it saved her having to trawl the shops and waste time making decisions. She settled on six matching cereal bowls (the bride was only on her husband's side) and ordered them to be sent the following day. Then she drifted through the linen department to check out the latest stock.

She really ought to be heading home but first she needed the ladies'. These lunches were Sisyphean affairs; her bladder was not what it had been. The store had just had a total makeover; she had not been in there for almost five years, since the building work had begun. But they wouldn't have shifted the cloakrooms, surely, halfway up the stairwells, in between floors.

She tidied her hair and checked her teeth, then sprayed on some Cartier cologne. She was only a two-minute cab ride from Eaton Square. These embassy functions were a crashing bore but Peregrine liked her to look her best so tonight she would wear the Saint Laurent satin as a foil to the emerald choker. In one of the cubicles the cistern flushed and someone was washing their hands beside her, though Tamara was too self-absorbed to spare a glance.

It was twenty to six; the store closed at seven. If it weren't for the function, she might have continued to browse. Filling in time was always a problem for a woman who'd never had a job, apart from sporadic fund-raising gigs for her husband. She picked up her bag and turned to go, then froze when she saw who (or what) was standing beside her.

Her heart started palpitating wildly. 'Kindly allow me to pass,' she said. Perry was right: she should not have worn so much bling. She could tell from the smile that things might well turn ugly and prayed for a saviour to intervene. But, by this time in the late afternoon, the ladies who lunch had gone home.

Tamara faced her nemesis alone, too petrified even to scream.

Her body was found by a security guard, doing his rounds before locking up. She was pinned to the wall beside the basins, the knife had gone in so deep. The look on her face was of frozen horror, her mouth a rictus of pure disbelief. Whoever had done this had virtually scared her to death. But for what purpose? She hadn't been robbed; her rings were intact and the Prada bag she had dropped remained unopened. She wasn't even young and pretty, and carried no mobile phone.

Panic ensued; the police were called but the body could not be moved till forensics had been. The big question was, had the cameras caught it? On this occasion they had, which at least was something. The store's refit had been long and costly. The entrance to the ladies' loo was guarded by cameras in all directions. Anyone entering or leaving should therefore be seen.

The evidence had to be passed to the police where it landed inevitably on Brewster's desk. Another bloody murder, he groaned. What the hell was going on?

He was working late that Tuesday night, scrutinising endless data in an attempt to check out Celeste's antecedents. Before he asked her further questions, he needed to know as much as he could if only to catch her out if she was lying. It wasn't a job he very much liked. He still hadn't totally made up his mind, was drawn to her in a way he found unnerving. He badly wanted to prove himself wrong but the process had to be gone through.

'Send it straight through,' he said wearily, when told that the tape was on its way. At least this time it might give them some sort of lead.

They gathered in the projection room in front of a magnifying screen, Brewster and his team of highly skilled experts. Coffee was brought and they all sat round, recording machines and notebooks to hand, intrigued to find out why the guard had been so freaked out.

The SOC report began with stomach-churning close-ups of the body, skewered to the wall and covered with blood, hands spread out as if imploring, face contorted with terror. The clothes were expensive, if overdone, the jewels the genuine thing. Yet nothing at all had been taken, said the report.

'Some kind of vengeance killing, do you think?' A jealous wife or over-importunate suitor.

They looked at each other and Brewster shrugged. She was surely too old to provoke a *crime passionnel*. But the savagery fitted with the Circle Line killings and, since it hadn't reopened yet, there could be a possible fit. Where else do you go when your stamping-ground is temporarily cordoned off? And the damage wrought by the knife was in a similar league. Even Brewster was finding it hard not to gag.

'OK,' he said, when they'd seen enough. 'Now let's look at the TV footage.' He drained his coffee mug, longing for whisky, and lit an illicit cigarette.

The film was clear and of excellent quality, though showed

only a flight of stone steps either way, leading up and down from the cloakroom positioned between the floors. For a very long time nothing happened at all. On the whole, as one of the team observed, shoppers use escalators rather than stairs.

'Or else the lifts. They're a lazy bunch.' Unless they wanted to pee.

They began to mutter among themselves until a figure popped into view, climbing the stairs in desperate search of the loo. Another long pause until she emerged.

'What do they do in there?' one asked. The cameras could not see beyond the closed doors.

'Breach of privacy,' explained the technician, embarrassed as if it were somehow his fault.

'I'd sooner watch paint dry,' said a weary detective.

'Wait,' ordered Brewster, suddenly alert. A slight dark figure had come into view, racing up the stairs on nimble feet.

It vanished abruptly into the cloakroom and thus was immediately lost to sight. Male or female? None of them knew; like a rat up a drainpipe, they said. After which there followed a lengthy pause, fifteen minutes or even more.

'Can't you speed this thing up?' asked the man from forensics.

Then, just as they were about to drop off, Lady Fermoy-French made her appearance.

She was in the cloakroom quite a while.

'Probably having a natter,' one said.

'A fag more likely,' said Brewster, lighting up.

The door at last opened but the figure which emerged was not that of Lady Fermoy-French but the previous arrival who'd been in there a good half-hour. Slim and dark was all they could make out; it might have been male or female. Whoever it was ran lightly up the stairs without ever glancing towards the cameras.

'Fast forward,' said Brewster urgently. But the rest of the tape was blank. That, apparently, was the end of the show.

'Nothing more happens till a later tape,' explained the technician. 'At six fifty-five the guard goes in. And finds Lady Whatshername skewered to the wall.'

'So now, at least, we have glimpsed the murderer. It can't have been anyone else. We just need formal identification. Run it through again,' said Brewster.

When the slim dark figure appeared on the stairs, Brewster leaned forward in his chair. 'Try for a close-up of the face,' he said. Something was tugging at the edge of his memory. Somewhere, not very long ago, he was almost certain he'd seen that person before.

The technician zoomed in as far as he could, then advanced the tape slowly, frame by frame. The killer appeared to have short dark hair which was all they could clearly make out. Next would come the interminable wait until Lady Fermoy-French appeared. And after that another long gap till they saw the killer again.

'This is no good. It's a total charade.' The team were all longing to call it a day. Yet they'd seemed so close to a genuine breakthrough.

'Wait,' said Brewster, suddenly inspired. 'How did the murderer leave the store? Walked on up to a higher floor then took the escalator down.'

'Or the lift.' But Brewster was no longer listening. He was hellbent on following a hunch.

By eleven p.m. he was almost dropping though still resolved not to quit. By then the forensics team had left and only the weary technician remained, valiantly checking through endless footage of film.

'I can't believe there's so much of it,' said Brewster. 'How many escalators do they have?'

'Fourteen now,' the man said glumly. 'Basement to the eighth floor.'

'Go on then,' said Brewster, dying for a drink but settling instead for a cigarette. He was starting to droop; he needed to keep a clear head.

And that's when he saw it, the face in the crowd that sent a bolt of electricity through him and made him doubt his sanity for a second. Calm and poised and exquisitely dressed, there was no mistaking that startling beauty as she rode the escalator down towards the ground floor.

'Again,' he said. They reversed the tape and ran it over and over until he was sure. It seemed she had been in the store at the time. Just as she'd been on the spot when Miranda was killed.

He sat and sweated, severely shaken. Although he'd initially suspected her, their latest meeting had given him pause. He had started to feel very drawn to her since that evening in the bar. Now, however, there was no turning back. He had a duty to perform. Having made his decision, he stubbed out his fag. Whatever romantic feelings he had, at heart he remained a high-principled cop. The job would always come first. The team had dispersed but that was tough luck. He put through the order all the same.

'Bring her in as fast as you can. Better take reinforcements.'

Part Three

34

It was six in the morning when the doorbell rang; Celeste was still asleep. She tried at first to ignore the sound, turned over and buried her face in the pillow, but the insistent banging of the knocker too convinced her there was someone at the door. She dragged herself over to the window. What she saw stopped her heart in her chest. Two police cars with flashing lights parked untidily right outside with four uniformed officers standing around. With a dog. She couldn't see who was at the door.

'Open up!' commanded a voice. She grabbed her robe and hurtled downstairs to try to stop the commotion. The last thing she needed was the neighbours in on the act.

There were two of them waiting in the porch, a man and a hard-faced woman.

'Celeste Forrester?' she asked, displaying her badge. 'We have a warrant for your arrest. Please get dressed and accompany us to the station.'

Celeste stared blankly. It must be a joke, though the woman showed not the slightest sign of humour. And the dog looked very threatening indeed.

'There must be some mistake,' she said. 'What is it I am supposed to have done?'

'You'll find out the details once we get to Cannon Street,' said the grim-faced woman.

Cannon Street was where Brewster worked. Celeste was suddenly gripped by terror. She had always suspected he didn't believe her; now it seemed that he was going to charge her.

'Give me five minutes,' she said with dignity and swept back up the stairs. She wouldn't bother waking Oberon, not that he would have cared. She didn't want Brewster knowing of his existence.

She came back regal and perfectly groomed. 'The detective inspector is a friend of mine,' she said.

The policewoman stared at her stonily. 'It was DI Brewster who sent us,' she said. She practically frogmarched Celeste to the car and pushed her in with a hand on her head. The dog came to sit beside her, baring its fangs.

Here they were again, face to face, though in quite different circumstances. Brewster was back in uniform, with a grave and inscrutable expression. He didn't even rise to greet her, but remained at his desk, engrossed in his work, without glancing up.

'Be seated,' said the lady cop, then stood to attention by the door. The atmosphere in the room could be cut with a knife.

'For goodness' sake,' Celeste said sharply. 'Won't somebody please tell me what this is about?' She was chilled to the bone by the atmosphere in the room.

His eyes, when at last he looked at her, were bloodshot and his face was drawn. He had been at his desk all night, since he issued the order. Before he spoke, the policewoman read out her rights. 'Do you want a solicitor?' she asked.

'Not till I know why I'm here,' said Celeste.

Brewster, who appeared to be sunk in thought, still had not uttered a word. Now he finally looked at her and she saw from his eyes that the news was bad.

'Murder in the first degree,' he said in a wooden voice.

'Miranda Perkins?' She couldn't believe it.

'Tamara, Lady Fermoy-French,' he replied.

He had to admire her brazen front and she did look a million dollars. He tried to remain detached but found it hard. Celeste just sat there, stupefied, unable to take it in. She certainly did have style, he gave her that.

'At approximately five fifty-five,' he said, 'yesterday evening at Peter Jones, you stabbed the victim to death with a kitchen knife.'

The colour drained from her flawless face; she positively gasped with surprise. Her great dark luminous eyes beseeched him to tell her it was a cruel joke. He found it hard to meet her gaze. She had somehow managed to break through his defences. Yet he had proof she had been there at that time.

'What have you to say?' he asked, switching on his recording machine.

'Nothing at all,' Celeste said stiffly. 'Except that I didn't do it. I have never even heard of the woman before.'

'I'm afraid we have it on film,' he said, his voice controlled and ice-cold. Please don't lie, he wanted to add. Or else I won't be able to help you.

Celeste absorbed this for several seconds. Then: 'Show me

207

the evidence,' she said. 'I didn't go near the store yesterday.' Which was not entirely true, in fact. He saw she knew that she was bending the truth.

'What time did you leave work?' he asked.

'Around five-thirty.'

'And went straight home?'

'I did,' she said. 'Baker Street to Sloane Square by way of Victoria.'

'Bringing you straight to Peter Jones.'

She couldn't deny it so said nothing.

'At approximately the time the murder was committed.'

Her eyes flashed sparks. 'But I didn't do it. I wasn't even in the store.'

'Can you prove it?' He badly wanted her to win. 'I'm afraid, Miss Forrester, the closed-circuit cameras do not lie.'

Celeste stayed silent; she had no defence. He saw her inwardly crumble. Her life had been hexed right from the start; she couldn't see any way out of it though by now, of course, she was figuring out what had happened.

'Any more questions?' She faced him full on, her beauty piercing him to the core.

'None,' said Brewster. 'Take her down. We are holding you in custody pending further inquiries.'

The cell was awful and smelt of Vim with an undercurrent of urine. They offered Celeste a solicitor again. She refused.

'What are you going to do?' asked the warder, a woman with a compassionate smile. 'Is there anyone we should notify that you are here?'

'No,' said Celeste. 'Except my boss. Tell him I won't be in for work and that I am very sorry.'

She wrote down his number, then contemplated. She really had no idea what to do for the best. She asked how long they would hold her there; a maximum of four days, said the warder, after which, by law, they were bound to let her go unless they formally charged her.

'I would like a change of clothes,' she said, 'if I'm going to be here that long.'

They gave her a prison overall and provided her with a toothbrush. They offered to pick up things from her house but she declined. She sat in silence and thought about it, trying to work out what to do, wondering how Oberon would cope when she didn't come home. And how he would ever find out where she had gone.

Brewster was also sitting in silence, still not entirely convinced of her guilt. If only the cameras hadn't caught her, she might well have got away with it. He knew he shouldn't ever think that way but, in this case, couldn't help it. She had seemed so defenceless in the interview room, vulnerable and afraid. And yet . . . he thought of what she had done, two women brutally hacked to death, probably several more. He wondered about her motivation and whether or not she was just plain mad. She certainly showed no sign of it but nor did she show remorse.

He wandered down to the detention block and studied her through the two-way glass. Even in prison regulation clothes she retained her dignity and poise. She sat staring into space, lost in an inner world. He would insist she get a lawyer, the very least he could do for her. The evidence against her was pretty damning.

35

He didn't emerge till almost noon, shattered by what had occurred. The adrenalin buzz he always got was invariably followed by a similar low. He wouldn't experience a high like that until he did it again. He showered and dressed, then went downstairs where he found the fridge almost empty. Provisions had sunk to an all-time low but tomorrow was Thursday when she did her big shop. Occasionally he requested things but didn't, as a rule, much care what he ate. He kept himself at minimum weight, could exist on very little.

He tried her door on the way back up but found it, as usual, locked. She was furious at the way he'd behaved, daring to tamper with her things, though still apparently hadn't twigged that he had a duplicate key. He didn't feel much like going out but was far too restless to settle. The weather was good so he thought he would go for a walk.

He didn't go far, just loafed around, confining himself to the

Chelsea backstreets, drawn like a homing pigeon to Peter Jones. The latest murder had made the headlines: 'Society hostess stabbed to death.' Her picture was there on all the newsstands, brassy and overdressed, with shifty eyes. He felt another adrenalin buzz; the bitch had certainly had it coming. People like her should not exist, putting on airs and flashing their wealth. Greedy, superficial and cruel. He knew her kind from his childhood.

Celeste was concerned about how he would cope but dared not risk the police discovering there was anyone else in the house. If she answered no questions, she might hold them off until the statutory four days were up and they had to let her go. They couldn't hold her indefinitely since she, for one, knew she wasn't guilty and therefore what evidence they had must be faulty. He'd been up to his tricks again, of course, had deliberately landed her in this mess out of spite. Though fully grown, he was still a spoilt child who flew into tantrums of thwarted rage if anyone tried to stand in his way or stop him doing what he liked.

She understood and sympathised. Nature had dealt him a very low blow and she'd been his champion since the day he was born. Their parents had grossly neglected him, had not looked after his welfare at all but turned their backs on a situation they were unable to handle. These days they would have been in court by now. Lately his behaviour had started to grow worse; she no longer knew how to control him. One of these days, if he hadn't already, he would go too far and they'd have to lock him up.

Julie was deeply immersed in her project and enjoying the research. Her main concentration was fixed on the Forresters now. There was definitely some sort of mystery there; the trail went cold right after their deaths and no one she'd found knew anything much about them. A theatrical knight and his glamorous lady; some scandal appeared to attach to them though what it had been she hadn't been able to uncover. In the end she sought out Rupert and asked him point-blank.

'What do you know about Esmée Morell?'

He looked up with an abstracted smile, busy writing his column. 'Very little, which is why I enlisted your help.'

'So why include her if her life is so obscure?'

'That's the whole thrust of the series. *Theatrical Legends*.'

She told him she had located the house, the scene of their celebrated salon, though hadn't established if anyone still lived there. 'Nobody ever answers the door and the place looks totally empty and neglected.'

'Have you thought of breaking in?' he asked, not entirely kidding. He had chosen Julie for her journalist's nose and gritty determination.

'I suppose I could set the place on fire and see who comes rushing out,' she said. Then gave him her brightest smile and returned to her desk. She wouldn't give up. She enjoyed a challenge, was determined to see the thing through. Was especially keen on the promised TV credit.

Later Rupert stopped by her desk and handed her a card. *Leonard Beamish – Actor*, it read. 'A fellow I know from the Garrick,' he said. 'Give him a buzz and say I told you to call.'

'Who is he?' asked Julie suspiciously. Not a name she had ever heard.

'One of the old-style theatricals who made his career in rep. Does endless bit parts on television. You'll certainly know the face.'

'What's the connection?'

'He acted with them. Played Puck at Stratford the season they met. Has always been a little in love with Esmée.'

Julie took the card impatiently. 'Anything else you've omitted to tell me?'

'I saw him the other night,' said Rupert. 'But it totally slipped my mind.'

When evening came and she still wasn't home, he really started to panic. She was out so little, especially at night, and never before without giving him warning. He was getting hungry now but had nothing to eat. With luck she had moved her big shop to tonight. He raided the fridge for the last bit of cheese and also uncovered an ancient tin of sardines. No bread, no eggs, not even milk. A very poor show altogether. He would order himself a takeaway if he could.

He paced the unlit reception rooms then made his nightly descent to the cellar. If he couldn't eat, he might just as well get plastered. His father may not have left him much but had, without doubt, possessed a superlative palate. He stood there, gazing at the once well-stocked shelves, now seriously depleted, selected a bottle of Grand Cru Muscat and ceremoniously pulled the cork. Of the very few pleasures allowed him in life, drinking came high on the list.

Because of the way they had lived and the fact that they were often on tour, his parents had seen very little of their children. Except on nights when they entertained and wanted to show them off, but after his infant years he'd been kept out of sight. Celeste would go down in her party frock, the image of her mother, they said, and do a dance or sing them a song; the visitors found her cute. He, alone and unseen on the stairs, could never have properly taken part but he'd loved the show of it all, which had seriously thrilled him. She had always been the favoured one, her daddy's darling, her mother's pet, which meant she had, inevitably, grown up a bitch.

Esmée Morell, with her fabled charm, underneath was a selfish and callous woman, caring only for her personal fame and the husband on whom she doted. It suited her to have a pretty daughter to emphasise her own glamorous looks, but as Celeste grew older she turned on her too. She raised her to be ruthless and hard, carelessly tossing her suitors aside, promising that there were better ones yet to appear. She studied their backgrounds with scrupulous care, only welcoming into her house the ones she considered the best, by which she meant rich.

Glass in hand, he went back upstairs and switched on the drawing-room lights. The grand piano on which she had played had been silent and shrouded all these years. The antiques were dusty, the mirrors tarnished. No one any longer polished the brass. It was all just junk; he could see that now, tawdry and meaningless possessions. If they sold the lot and moved away, they could have a very much better lifestyle. But he was too scared to consider such a change or even stand up and face the world. He blamed it all on his mother.

36

The summer was showing no signs of letting up. Beth felt in serious need of a break. Richard had asked them to his house in France and she desperately wanted to go.

'Any time will suit me,' he said. 'I plan to be there all summer.'

Jane and Alastair were also invited; it could be a lot of fun. Richard was an exemplary host provided they let him get on with his work. He was putting together an autumn exhibition.

'Bring Imogen too.' The house was huge and Richard was her godfather.

'I can't,' she wailed. 'The show will still be running and they'd never allow me time off.' Not that she would want it, either; she was proud of being in such a great production. Every performance was fully sold out right to the end of the season.

'Good,' said Duncan, though with a grin. 'You can look after the dogs.'

'Oh, darling,' said Beth. 'Will you be all right?' She hated the thought of her stuck in London on her own. 'Perhaps you ought to ask Alice to stay.' She could even bring that awful Julie. In this hot weather they might enjoy having access to a garden.

'Mum,' said Imogen, her regular cry. 'I'm not a child any more.'

But they still hadn't caught the Circle Line killer and there'd just been another horrendous murder in, of all unlikely places, a classy department store. Though Beth was too smart to mention that. Her daughter was right; she had to live her own life.

When she had still not returned by morning, he came out in a cold sweat. From childhood she had looked after him and now was his only lifeline. He was seriously hungry, with a splitting head, the result of too much wine. He looked for an aspirin without success. He couldn't believe she would just walk out, despite the number of times she had threatened to. She loved him really; in his heart he knew that. She would not abandon him now. As he would never abandon her, even were he to have the option. They were joined at the hip and always would be. Both had grown up knowing that.

Then he remembered how he'd trashed her room and damaged some of her precious things. He had the right: in a way they were his things too. If he wanted to wear his mother's hats, it wasn't for her to interfere. But this time he had possibly gone too far. He remembered shattering her crystal bottles and grinding the shards into the beautiful rug. He gnawed his finger and thought about it. If he knew where to look, he would go and find her. Until he remembered the latest thing he had done.

He popped round the corner and bought a paper, something he'd never dared do before; just handed the man the right change and hurried away. On the second page was a tiny item

218

in the right-hand column of just-breaking news. 'Suspect Held' was all it said. But he knew.

'My mum's had this totally mad idea,' said Imogen on the phone to Alice. 'They are off to France in a couple of days and don't want me here on my own. She suggested you might come over and stay. Bring Julie too. You could help with the dogs.'

'Whatever's got into her?' asked Alice, who'd known Beth Hardy most of her life. 'She can't still imagine you need a babysitter.'

'You know what she's like.'

'I do,' said Alice, but the thought of that lovely spacious house was enticing; the garden too at this time of year.

'It's the murders,' said Imogen. And today's nasty news of the second lot of terrorist bombs. Even though they hadn't gone off, London was now a very dangerous place.

'Tamara, Lady Fermoy-French,' mocked Alice, 'sounds rather like Danny La Rue. Out of one of the glossy mags, slashed in a ladies' loo.' Something about it was deliciously absurd. Especially in a department store. Neither of them could help chuckling.

'She was ordering something from a wedding list,' said Imogen. 'The essence of the bourgeoisie. Which only goes to prove you can't be too careful.'

Exactly her mother's thinking, of course, which was why she'd suggested that the girls should move in. They discussed it further and Alice agreed; staying with Imogen was always fun and would also mean a slightly shorter journey to work.

'What about Julie?'

'I'll ask her,' said Alice. 'But don't be surprised if she says no.' Julie had not been the best of company since getting involved in the Hallmark series. She was out all hours or else reading late. Her bedroom smelt like an ashtray.

Survival had to be his first concern now that he knew she was not coming back; not, at least, before he had starved to death. He might have overplayed his hand, just hadn't thought through the repercussions; wanted to scare her and let her know how far he was willing to go. He had been alarmed by those two young women – three, he now remembered; there had been a fair one too. It seemed they were closing in from all sides. He had seen the tall one several more times on her way to the National Theatre. It surely could not be coincidence that two of them, on quite separate occasions, had been standing right outside his house, showing rather too much interest.

Later he'd seen all three together and they'd paused to watch his act and laugh. Admiration he took in his stride but laughter he could not cope with. He did what he did for the adulation, had absorbed the need with his mother's milk. They hadn't really seen him, not at any of those times, but he had most certainly taken them in. And would not forget their faces in a hurry. He closed his eyes and the blood was there, swirling around in his consciousness, making his breath come in short sharp gasps, the palms of his hands cold and clammy. The spots were gathering in front of his eyes; if he didn't sit down he would faint. Later, he'd feel the ache in his groin and know he was ready to do it again. Thus it had been since the accident in the house.

Rather to Imogen's surprise, Julie said she would love to move in. She was tired of the stifling heat in central London. It was also only a walk away, over the hill from the *Daily Mail*, closer even from the flat she shared with Alice.

'It'll be all right. She's improved a lot.' Alice was well aware of her flatmate's failings.

'Don't worry,' said Imogen. 'There's bags of room. And, to tell the truth, I like her far more than I did.'

Julie had cut her partying down, was showing a slightly more serious side. Had got them watching old films with her at weekends. She was slightly starstruck by Imogen's house but dutifully pulled her weight by walking the dogs.

After she died the police had come but had managed to keep the press away because of his age and the manner of her death. There had been a thorough investigation after which he had spent three years in a home until his sister turned twenty-one and reclaimed him. They had taught him nothing; he had rebelled. They'd been glad to see the back of him when she had agreed to act as his legal guardian. Slowly, as other stories took their place, the rumours had started to fade away. His father died in a matter of months, of a broken heart it was said. Nothing was proved and no charges brought because he was then still a minor.

Celeste had dropped out of acting school though, in truth, she had never really shared the gift. He was the one who, had he been able, was born to perpetuate the family name. A reason for his endless rage. Through a freak of nature he had been denied his birthright.

There was a Marks & Spencer in the King's Road which had to be his initial target. He was all fired up to attempt the difficult mission. After doing deep-breathing exercises, he took his bag and donned his dark glasses then set off in pursuit of something to eat. Milk and bread were the main essentials; cheese and fruit, too, if he had enough cash. He had some savings of his own but had never before had to fend for himself. He had no idea how much things cost; had never been shopping before. But people did it, it was part of life. He would just be careful to choose the shortest queue.

37

She worried about how he'd cope alone, having never before had to do so. In the eighteen years they had been on their own they had virtually never been parted. Except, of course, for his years in an institution. She thought of him now, in that tomb of a house, packed with memories he'd sooner forget, with no way of finding out where she was or if she had simply walked out. It had crossed her mind to do so any number of times; there had been occasions, as he grew older, when he'd almost driven her crazy. But the bond between them was very strong. Both knew in their hearts that, no matter what happened, she would always be there to protect him.

He'd be traumatised when she didn't come home, trapped in his own living purgatory, marooned with nothing to eat or drink, unable even to call for help or pop next door to a neighbour. She wondered if she should spill the beans but then they would only arrest him. And this time round he would get a much heavier sentence. She couldn't forget what a sweet kid he'd been. Only circumstances had caused him to change.

The night in the cell had been horrendous. She couldn't imagine how she must look. The friendly warder brought her a tray of breakfast.

'How long are they going to keep me here?'

'Until they have some answers,' said the warder. 'Four days is the legal maximum without a formal charge.'

Four days was too long to leave him alone. There was no predicting what he might do. She wished there was somebody she could trust. She had never felt more alone.

'When do I get to see DI Brewster?'

'When he's good and ready,' was the reply.

She was right; he thought she was guilty. The idea appalled her.

Brewster had been unable to sleep. He could not get her out of his mind. Although it was he who had issued the warrant, he still found it hard to believe she had killed. It wasn't only her fragile looks; everything about her was privileged – the way she moved and dressed and spoke. It simply didn't add up. They brought her back to the interview room for another confrontation but this time he found it hard to meet her eye. Any rapport they might have established had died when he had her arrested.

He asked more of his repetitive questions; she answered the same as before. She stuck to her guns; it seemed he could not touch her. She had not been in Peter Jones when that woman was killed. Nor had she murdered Miranda either, despite being on the spot. There was something she was holding back; he

224

couldn't think what it could be. If only she'd open her heart to him, he would do all it took to save her.

Having failed to get anything out of Celeste, Brewster arranged to meet her employer, the doctor for whom she had worked for eleven years. Dr Rousseau received him in his elegant office, stylishly dressed and impeccably groomed. Brewster was struck by the softness of his hands. He was courteous and engagingly French as well as one hundred per cent on her side. No, he said, there could be no doubt. The woman he'd worked with so long could not be a killer.

'She has far too much *savoir faire*,' he said, 'to put herself in that sort of position. A lover, maybe, but – *tiens* – another employee?' It was clear he was more than a little in love with her.

They could find no link between the two women beyond shared office space. The staff confirmed that they had never been close. Their social backgrounds were worlds apart; there was no need to say more.

What was her background, Brewster wanted to know. What did she do before working for him? The doctor gave an eloquent shrug. It was so long ago he could not remember. Would it be on the files? Why, no, he said. Receptionists didn't have records.

'And her home life?'

That was the baffling part for such a sensational woman. 'None, as far as I am aware.' He only knew that she lived alone in what had once been her family home. She seemed to have little social life. Kept herself very much to herself. A shocking waste. Both men agreed on that.

*   *   *

On the way to the car, it came back to him. The night he had walked Celeste home. He had half expected her to ask him in; it was Saturday night and not yet nine. She had made an effort to look her best so why had she changed so abruptly? Both were single and unattached; at least, that was what he had understood. And he had been offering the hand of friendship, feeling he'd been too tough the first time round. They'd been chatting easily till they reached her street when all of a sudden she held out her hand, told him she'd be all right from that point and hurried off without another word.

Baffled, he'd wandered along behind her and stood on the other side of the street, regretting not being a touch more assertive instead of letting her go like that. Which was when he'd seen the flicker of light from a window on the top floor. There was obviously someone else in the house, so why had she not said so?

He went back to see her in her cell and asked the question point-blank. He might be intruding but to hell with it. She was under arrest for suspected murder. If she didn't answer his questions, he wanted to know why.

'Does anyone share your house?' he asked. She was looking drawn and unwell.

'No,' she said. 'I told you that. When are you going to let me go? It is very inconvenient being in here.'

'But after you left me, I saw a light. I stood outside your house for a while. To check that you were all right.' He felt slightly foolish.

She stared at him blankly but didn't respond except that her eye was twitching again. It was almost like a lie-detector. She needed to learn to control it.

'Are you suggesting I imagined it?' He had an irresistible urge to shake her. He wished she would get a grip on herself. Her life was on the line. 'Or a ghost maybe?'

'Perhaps,' she said. 'The house is very old.'

38

The voice that answered when Julie called was petulant and shrill.

'Yes?' it said, as though he were hard of hearing.

'Mr Beamish?' It couldn't be him; by now he must be as old as the hills.

'Who wants him?' he asked, suddenly sounding guarded.

Julie acted on inspiration. 'I am calling on behalf of Hallmark,' she said.

That did it. Immediately the petulance faded. 'Ooh,' he said, sounding decidedly camp. 'Tell me more.'

Julie grinned. They were all much the same. The smell of big bucks brought them running. 'I'm working on a new series,' she said. 'And was rather hoping you might be able to help me.'

The rest was easy. He agreed to meet and invited her over to his Wandsworth flat. 'Ought I involve my agent?' he asked.

'No,' said Julie. 'Not at this stage.' She didn't want to risk losing him. 'I'd far rather talk to you first, if you don't mind.'

He could see her whenever she liked, he said, so they made a date for the following week. For her it would mean taking time off work but this was more important. At last she seemed to be getting somewhere. She prayed he'd deliver the goods.

The morning after her lunch with Margaret and the shock of the bombs that had failed to go off, Ellie was due to go and pick up Wilbur. She had packed some clothes for him in a bag, with slippers because of his injured hip, and asked the porter to kindly get her a taxi. First, though, she rang the hospital to check that everything was on schedule.

'One moment,' said the duty nurse. 'Sister would like a word.'

Ellie hung on for several minutes until the sister came on the line. 'I'm afraid,' she said, 'there are slight complications. He won't be leaving today.' And made an appointment for Ellie to see the consultant.

'Something's come up,' said the affable man, twinkling with bonhomie. 'The bones have fused quite splendidly and he's able to walk with the help of two sticks. Soon, if he keeps up the exercises, he shouldn't have any more trouble.'

'But?' said Ellie, keen to get to the point.

'We need to do some more tests. The sugar content of his blood is high. It seems he may have contracted diabetes.'

'Why would that be?' Ellie asked. It had never been diagnosed before.

'He is overweight. He will have to make drastic diet changes.'

'Which means?' she said.

'That he'll have to stay in for at least another week. Maybe more. Until we have regulated his blood sugar level.'

230

Something disloyal clicked in her brain and she heaved a secret sigh of relief. Though she did her best to conceal it from the doctor.

Wilbur, however, seemed not to mind; he was already into his poker game and, as usual, made her feel she was intruding. 'Better to find out now,' he said. And get it free on the NHS. All he thought about was money. She had started to despise him.

So what was she going to do for a week? Wilbur apparently wasn't bothered. She could entertain herself, was becoming an expert. More to the point, she still had his cheques and the Paris tickets that had been deferred. She kissed him lightly then hurried away to share the good news with Margaret.

Amy was getting on Margaret's nerves with her selfish impositions. It was late July and the kids were under her feet. Margaret considered she more than pulled her weight; it wasn't within a granny's brief to look after them all the time. She read to them and took them out and stood in whenever her daughter-in-law went away with her work. But she was allowed a life of her own, which they often seemed to forget.

Much of her time she spent in the garden, especially nice at this time of year, and at night she had a lot of books to catch up with. Although she had dropped the local reading group there was an on-line one she liked in Saturday's *Times*. She was currently working her way through Thomas Hardy.

But when the phone rang and it was Ellie, she was more than willing to be disturbed. Yesterday's lunch had cheered her up and renewed her appetite for life. Ellie filled her in briefly on Wilbur's health then made her bold suggestion. A week in Paris, all expenses paid. How about it?

Margaret didn't need to think twice; it was just the tonic she needed. Although she insisted on paying for herself. We'll discuss that later, said Ellie. It was Saturday morning; they would leave on Monday. Margaret rushed off to sort through her clothes and drop a message of false regret to her importunate daughter-in-law. Ellie, delighted, went out to buy a guidebook

By the following day she had still not come home though news of the latest murder was all over the papers. There was a lot about Lady Fermoy-French and the terrible way she had met her death but all the police were reported as saying was that they were holding a suspect. No further details, but of course he guessed what must have happened. He didn't know what he would do if they came to the house. Sooner or later she was bound to crack, which meant he must make a contingency plan. Once she could prove she was in the clear, they were bound to start delving deeper. He didn't know what he would do when they came, apart from refusing to open the door. And in that event it could only be a question of time before they returned with a warrant.

Although he missed her and feared for her safety, he had also always resented her. She was able to hold down a job and live a more or less normal life. Frustrated, as he usually was, he read her mail and spied on her, scared that one day she'd have had enough and leave him. In the past two weeks he had seen her with two men, neither of whom he knew anything about. Both appeared to be after her; one had been hanging round the house. Without him she might have had a future, some children, got married, been happy. But what sort of man would take her on with him as part of the package?

He paced the house with nothing to do, not daring to risk

going out. He was too upset to do anything much except drink. From time to time he went to the window in the hope of seeing her on her way home but the quiet street, as usual, was deserted. When night came, he dared not switch on the lights but huddled alone in his attic room, biting his nails as he desperately searched for a plan. The time to leave would be in the night, though he had no idea where he'd go.

He was far too strung up to be able to sleep but when bedtime came and she still wasn't home, he decided to give it a go. He went to the window for one last look and his heart almost stopped in his chest when he saw a police car parked outside.

39

Beth had popped out for some last-minute shopping. They were catching the afternoon ferry to Dieppe. Most of the packing had already been done. Duncan was getting the car filled up. Imogen sat on the stairs with the dogs, waiting for her new housemates to arrive.

'Now try not to do too much partying,' said Beth, when she bustled back, arms full. 'Remember you need your beauty sleep. And that goes for all of you.' She need not worry too much about Imogen, who'd be at the theatre six nights a week, though she still didn't like the thought of her travelling home alone. She worried more about Julie, who had always struck her as brash and shallow. Not an obvious friend for Alice whose mother, she knew, felt much the same. Still, she was glad the girls were willing to housesit her daughter. Not that she'd put it like that, of course. Imogen would have killed her.

'The same applies to you,' said Imogen. 'Be careful on those

French roads.' She almost wished she was going too but would have more fun, she was pretty sure, staying here unchaperoned with her friends. Alice looked forward to the washing machine while Julie was planning to perfect her tan. Though she was sorry the dishy stepfather wouldn't be around.

'Now, be sure and ring us if there's anything at all.'

'Stop worrying, Mum,' said Imogen. 'Go and have that well-earned rest and forget all about the shop and me. Remember, if all else fails, we have the dogs.'

'I know, I know, but you know how I am.'

'I do,' said Imogen, hugging her.

Duncan took her aside before they left. 'Don't forget to phone,' he said. 'I know she fusses but you're still the centre of her life.'

'I know,' said Imogen. 'I promise to behave. Now go and get on that blasted ferry or else you'll ruin our orgy for tonight.'

She was waving them off when the girls arrived, spilling boxes and packages out of the cab, Julie lugging a crate of red wine, Alice carrying a pot plant.

'Oh dear,' said Beth, as they drove away.

'Shut up and relax,' said her ever-loving husband.

'What do you want to do next?' asked Imogen, after they'd done the Portobello Road and eaten lunch at the local Pizza Express.

'When are you due at the theatre?' asked Julie, still envious of Imogen's glitzy life.

'Not till six. We have plenty of time. We could always take a stroll down Kensington High Street.'

'I can do that in the week,' said Julie. It was where the paper was situated. 'If you don't mind, I'd prefer to go back to Chelsea.'

'Fine with me,' said placid Alice who was always easy, what-ever it was. There was nothing she wanted to buy but so what? She liked hanging round in this jolly threesome, was glad her two friends were finally starting to click

'Do you mind if we don't go shopping?' Julie astonished them both. She was like a magpie when it came to clothes; there were things in her wardrobe with the price-tags still on. Alice had never known her pass up such a chance before.

'What is it you want to do?' asked Imogen, who had no pref-erence either way. It was fun to hang out with Alice and her flatmate. Though she'd had her doubts about Julie at first, she was rapidly starting to like her a lot. She was full of zip and always raring to go.

'Some detective work, if you really don't mind. I have found out at last where the Forresters actually lived.'

There was a police car sitting outside the house, though it drove away when the girls arrived. Probably having their lunch, said Julie, and now off to watch the cricket. They drifted past but the house looked abandoned, even more than it had before. The brass on the door badly needed a polish and the mat was a dis-grace. There were buttercups and grass growing up between the tiles in the porch.

'It's a shame,' said Alice, 'that they've let it go. It must have been glorious in its day.' She imagined it with its windows agleam and a footman waiting by the open door as the carriages rolled up and the guests arrived.

'Hang on a minute!' said Imogen suddenly. 'I swear I've been to this house before.' She stood quite still till it all came back. The night of the bombs and that woman, Celeste. Only that time she'd only seen it for a few minutes. 'I don't think

237

I ever heard her last name. I'll ask my mum next time we speak.'

'Did you do anything about finding their graves?' Alice asked. Seeing the actual house made it suddenly more intriguing.

'No,' said Julie. 'There hasn't been time.' But she told them about Leonard Beamish. 'I'm going to see him on Monday,' she said. 'He sounds a bit of an oddity.'

'I would guess they are buried in Brompton Cemetery,' said Imogen. 'We could check that out. Or else at the actors' church in Covent Garden.'

'What are you going to do?' asked Alice, falling in with Julie's purposeful stride. They had walked the length of the block and now were heading back.

'I shall ring the bell and play it by ear which seems to make the best sense. If there's no one there, I shall leave my card and hope that someone will contact me.' If that should fail, she was hoping Beamish might come through.

Julie rang the bell and, when nothing happened, scribbled a note on her business card and dropped it through the tarnished letter box.

Alice sat on the warm brick wall and closed her eyes in the afternoon sun. 'It must have been wonderful in the old days, living in such an elegant street, surrounded by artists and writers.'

Julie and Imogen swapped a glance. There went Alice, the dreamer, again. Still, she did have a point. It seemed ludicrous that such a magnificent house should be left to decay.

They had finally left. He had checked all morning and at last the police car had driven off. He had no idea what they could have wanted since he hadn't opened the door. But they'd sat there in shifts throughout the night, presumably ringing the bell at times. He didn't know since he'd been upstairs in the attic. Now, however, it was afternoon and the watch had not been replaced. It might be because of the weekend or else they had simply given up. Either way, he was glad they had gone and was able to breathe more freely. He couldn't stand being cooped up like this so would head straight back to his usual patch. The South Bank was crowded on Saturday nights. There had been more bombs but no one seemed terribly scared; he hoped to make a killing.

Still no word from her but he'd given up. Sooner or later they would let her go or else they would have to charge her. He showered and shaved, feeling much better, then packed his bag for the evening shift. The itch was beginning to get much worse and would soon be beyond control

He was daily growing more confident since he'd crossed the barrier of learning to shop. He had counted his money and had enough to keep him going for a week or so. He had never done anything for himself; all his life he had been looked after. Those in the know still thought him subnormal but nothing was actually wrong with his brain. Celeste knew that, which was why they stuck together. He had never cooked but had often watched her; knew how to heat a frying pan and use the microwave. And now he knew he could also shop, the walls of his prison were really starting to fall.

Wearing dark glasses, he checked the street in case the cops had returned. What he saw instead, with a sickening jolt, was something that stopped him dead in his tracks. All three harpies were right outside, one of them sitting on his wall.

40

Suicide bombers had struck again, this time with no casualties since none of the bombs went off. The police put it down to incompetence. Somebody somewhere had royally boobed which meant they now had a number of leads and were rapidly closing in. The gang had been caught on CCTV, easily recognised and now under siege. The media frenzy was at its height; Londoners, glued to their screens, were watching it avidly. Brewster, whose area of expertise it was, was in overall charge of the operation. Burgess had also come into his own and was out there controlling the crowds.

It meant that they'd had to put on hold the murder inquiry they were working on. The suspect they'd taken in was still in detention. Despite the fact that they had her on film, she still refused to co-operate, and, without more evidence, they might not be able to charge her. Before this latest emergency they'd done all they could to reason with her yet, unbelievably, she was still refusing to talk. Burgess had been to the house with a team but no one appeared to be living there now. If it weren't for the suspect's original statement, and the fact it was there they had picked her up, the place might well have been derelict, it looked so completely uncared for. All the windows were firmly shut, unusual at this time of year. The paint was flaking; the window glass looked wobbly in the frames. The team had taken a quick look round but, until they'd been issued with a formal warrant, there was nothing they could do to gain admittance.

Remembering the flicker at the upstairs room, Brewster put a round-the-clock watch on the house but no one was spotted going in or out during that time. Every room remained in darkness; nobody ever answered the bell. In the end he called the surveillance off. The patrolmen were needed for the terrorist round-up. Why she refused to co-operate, he still couldn't figure out. Nor could Dr Rousseau explain though he was obviously loyally on her side.

What troubled him most was his own state of mind; his head was in a turmoil. Something about her wistful beauty had really succeeded in getting to him. He was developing stronger feelings than any he'd experienced since his youth. He feared it might be the first stirrings of love. He hoped not.

Sir Peregrine Fermoy-French was a fop in the old Edwardian style. Thirty years older than his trophy wife, he still affected the air of a man who spends most of his time at his club. Brewster was ushered in by a maid who'd have taken his hat if he'd had one. The baronet stood by the empty fireplace sipping a glass of dry sherry. He pointedly didn't offer one to Brewster. Nor did he invite him to sit.

'Mind if I take the weight off my feet?' Brewster wasn't

impressed by this snobbery nonsense. An inherited title did not equate with a serving member of Her Majesty's forces, especially one who'd been wounded in active service.

Sir Peregrine grunted but could hardly refuse, though he still didn't offer Brewster a drink. Not that he would have accepted one while on duty. He pulled out his notebook to underline that this visit was strictly official.

'Tell me,' he asked, 'can you think of anyone who might have wanted to harm your wife?'

'Almost everyone, I'd say, old chap. Beginning with yours truly.' If that was humour, it left Brewster cold. The man was vile; he wished he could run him in.

'Chapter and verse, please,' he asked him formally, tapping the notebook with his pen. 'I understand Lady Fermoy-French was a bit of a socialite.'

'You can say that again.' Sir Peregrine laughed as though it were not his wife who was under discussion. His dead wife, what's more. He might have shown some respect. 'She was out so much I rarely saw her, not that it made much difference. The stuffing went out of the marriage a long time ago.'

'How did she spend her time?' asked Brewster, refusing to be drawn. From the little he knew of the latest victim, she had been well matched with this ghastly man.

'Oh, the usual stuff. You know what they're like,' said the baronet, topping up his glass. 'Shopping, gossiping, playing bridge. Sitting on endless committees frittering time.'

'Would you say she was popular?'

'Hardly,' he said, with a sniff of disdain. 'Her sole claim to fame was as my wife.'

Brewster paused then cut to the chase. This was going nowhere; the man was a boor and a fool. If there'd been a way to implicate him, he'd have done it like a shot. Patiently, he tried another tack though it really hurt him to do so.

'Does the name Celeste Forrester ring any bells?' He tensed as he spoke the name aloud.

The baronet, barely listening, shook his head. 'I could never tell any of her friends apart; they were all as vacuous as each other. Now I must fly.' He looked at his watch. 'Lunch in the City with my broker.'

A hollow man with a celluloid heart. Brewster gave him his card. 'If you think of anything, let me know.' But he knew he was wasting his time.

Brewster had reached another dead end. He felt angry and frustrated. Despite the fact that they had her on film, he could find no link between her and the victim. Yet the peculiar viciousness of the attack bore all the signs of the work of the Circle Line killer.

41

The address in Wandsworth was a purpose-built block, 1930s and slightly seedy but decidedly atmospheric. Julie arrived there with time to spare to get the feel of the neighbourhood and savour its ambience. A natural journalist from birth, she knew the importance of getting the details right. She rang the doorbell precisely at ten and a voice she recognised from her call demanded, in stentorian tones, who was there.

'Julie,' she said, then, remembering her cover, 'from Hallmark Television.'

He buzzed her in and was waiting to greet her, a gnomish man in a shiny suit with a poorly disguised toupee. Leonard Beamish was as she'd imagined, an ageing Puck who had failed to fulfil his potential.

'Enchanted, I'm sure.' He ushered her through to a minute sitting room where a couple of couches occupied most of the space. He offered her tea and went to make it, leaving her free to look round and make herself at home. Despite the weather, the windows were shut and the atmosphere decidedly musty. It was like a time-warp from an earlier age. There were antimacassars on the chairs and a rubber plant badly in need of a dust. The walls were covered with fading sepia photos.

'Ah,' he said, coming up behind her. 'Me in starrier days.' He was holding a tray with a dainty cloth, a teapot in a knitted cosy, a couple of Jubilee cups and saucers and a plate of ginger biscuits. He placed it all fussily on the table and plumped up the cushions for her to sit.

Today she had taken the wise precaution of toning down her image. Instead of her usual garish persona, with garments deliberately chosen to clash, she was dressed like a sober office worker in her plain grey interview suit. Her hair, instead of its usual spikes, was brushed back smoothly behind her ears and the whole effect was enhanced by black-framed glasses. They'd have died in the office to see her like this but Julie was an instinctive pro. She needed to put this man at his ease before starting on the questions.

She glanced again at the photographs, in most of which he appeared. Clowning around or striking a pose, he had clearly missed the dramatic roles because of his lack of stature and high-pitched voice. His hair was faded but had once been red; his eyes were pale blue and bloodshot. As he poured the tea she smelt peppermint on his breath.

'So,' he said, once they were settled, politely passing the ginger nuts. 'What is it you want from me? I'm all ears.'

Which he was indeed, an odd little man with the cosmetic smile of an erstwhile imp whose dentures didn't quite fit. Julie had brought a fat folder with her to emphasise her professional status. She sensed she might be stepping on delicate ground.

246

'It's good of you to see me,' she said. 'And of course you will be reimbursed for your time.' Rupert had not mentioned expenses but she felt it struck an authentic note. She was having fun working herself into the role.

'No need,' he said, and his smile was broad. He sat like a nervous interviewee, fingers entwined in his lap.

He thinks I am offering him work, she thought, wondering how she could let him down without too much damage to his ego. She flicked through the file while she organised her thoughts, fearing to mess things up at this crucial stage.

'I wonder if you could tell me,' she said, trying to sound as impersonal as she could, 'what you know about the actress, Esmée Morell.'

His eyes bulged and his jaw sagged slightly; she feared he might swallow his plate. Whatever he knew, it was clear she had caught him off guard.

'Goodness,' he said. 'You have got me there. It's been years since I even thought about her. What exactly is it you are after?'

Julie dramatically lowered her glasses and looked him directly in the eye. 'As much as you can remember,' she said. 'In particular, when and how she came to die.'

'Mum,' said Imogen, when Beth rang in to check how things were going. 'What was the name of that woman you had here for lunch?'

'What woman?' asked Beth, in holiday mode, who entertained a lot.

'The beautiful one you met on a train. On 7/7, the morning the bombs went off.'

'Oh,' said Beth. 'Celeste Forrester. You've met her a couple of times.'

'What do you know about her life apart from living in a very big house on her own?'

'Almost nothing. She doesn't say much.' They mainly talked about the murder and the cop.

'Do you happen to know who her parents were? If her mother was an actress?'

'No,' said Beth. 'Though it wouldn't surprise me. What's this all about?'

'Just something Julie's doing for the paper. I'm helping her with research.'

'So it's working out?' Beth was relieved though hoped the awful Julie wouldn't lead her astray.

'Absolutely. We're getting on fine. She's got a wicked sense of humour.'

We may have cracked it, she wrote in a note which she left on the kitchen table for Julie. Since Celeste was indeed a Forrester, they must be getting close.

Esmée Morell, a name from the past. At first that was all he said. Julie knew, though, from his instant pallor, that he was holding things back. She held her breath and said nothing at all while he sank into a deep reverie. He gulped his tea, then scratched his head; she feared for the safety of the toupee. His eyes were focused on the middle distance. He seemed to forget she was there.

'Esmée Morell,' he eventually said, and she had the feeling he was faking fast. 'The most charismatic woman I've ever known.'

The plunge taken, he turned to face her, almost defiant in his stance. The colour had returned to his cheeks; the pale-blue eyes were fired. He had, however, misjudged Julie, who almost always gave better than she got.

'Mind if I go to the little girl's room?' she asked.

The bathroom was another cliché, though in no way was she surprised. Huge framed portraits of long-dead monarchs, interspersed with signed photos of stars. One of them, right above the cistern, was signed flamboyantly with Esmée's name, with a row of kisses, and inscribed to 'dearest Lennie'.

Julie discreetly washed her hands and plastered her hair back behind her ears. She was definitely getting somewhere now; felt she might be closing in on the truth.

42

As a child he had been adorable, with his soulful eyes and appealing smile and a wistfulness that practically broke your heart. Celeste was ten when her brother was born and right from the start, as a matter of course, had made herself responsible for his welfare. The rejoicing in the house had been great; at last the son and heir had arrived. Madame had fulfilled her ultimate dream; her family was now complete. Trumpets sounded and the press went wild but, rather than putting her nose out of joint, the son's arrival helped to aggrandise Celeste. With the baby carriage to push around, she found herself even more in the spotlight. The christening was held at St Paul's, Covent Garden where plaques to both her parents were now displayed. They would, of course, have preferred the Abbey but, as things turned out, that was not to be. The hubbub that heralded Oberon's birth was, ironically, the start of their gradual decline.

Most of theatrical London was there, including a handful of megastars who flew in specially for the occasion, two of them as godparents. Esmée, already slightly wobbly on her feet, had stood at the font in one of her hats and her vibrant trill had resounded throughout the church. The paparazzi were waiting outside when the band of luvvies spilled into the graveyard and Sir Edward voiced some well-chosen words to welcome his longed-for son. Another Forrester. Everyone cheered. May he continue the illustrious thespian line.

The rejoicing, alas, had not lasted long. The idyll rapidly faded. Despite his beauty, as the baby grew the realisation had gradually dawned. He was not quite as perfect as he had seemed at first. Esmée, almost demented with grief, abruptly turned her back on the child, banishing him to the upper floors and trying to pretend he didn't exist. At first she admitted the fault was hers though she later rescinded that story. She'd had German measles which was no big deal. She had ceased her drinking for the full nine months. All it had been was an accident of fate. Later he had come to share that opinion. But it *was* her fault, there could be no dispute. She should never have let him be born. It was no life at all for any living creature, especially one with his intelligence and looks. The biggest waste, though, was of his inherited talent.

Celeste gradually took over the care of him, along with a battalion of nursery staff, none of whom stayed long out of pure frustration. Her parents were very seldom home, being usually either on tour or performing in London, and neither now would acknowledge their only son. Used, as they were, to adulation, flawed perfection was something they could not accept. Celeste was too young to understand quite what a burden she had taken on: a lifetime's devotion that ended her own career.

252

Now, as she languished in her cell, she reflected on all those wasted years. If only her mother could have come to terms with what was no more than a quirk of fate, her own life might have been happier too and the ultimate tragedy avoided.

This time he'd exceeded even himself, landing her in a situation from which she could not see any easy escape. Short of blowing the whistle on him, something she was resolved not to do, she would have to remain in custody until they formally charged her. Or let her go; without evidence they could not hold her for more than four days. And though Brewster said he had visual proof, in fact he was mistaken.

Beamish had acted with both the Forresters, starting at Stratford in 1969 in Trevor Nunn's acclaimed *Midsummer Night's Dream*. She played Titania, Forrester Oberon and Beamish a critically applauded Puck. He was just seventeen at the time; it was his first break.

'That was the season they got together,' said Beamish. 'My God, she was hot. She played her in a diaphanous gown, which was pretty daring, considering her age. The magic between them was electrifying. Sex just oozed from their every pore. By the end of the season Esmée was pregnant. They married two months later.'

His eyes were misty with a strong emotion. He'd been more than a little in love with her himself; the effect, he said, she'd had upon most men.

'Tell me about her,' said Julie gently, careful not to destroy the mood. She switched on the small recording device she had brought.

Leonard Beamish was off in a trance; the words came tumbling out. 'The attraction between them was sex incarnate. The audiences lapped it up. It was like the pull between Burton and Taylor. I have never seen anything like it before or since.'

'And the child?' At last she was making progress.

'A daughter. Celeste or something fancy like that. Conveniently born in a gap between productions.'

Julie waited but he had dried up, back in his own emotional past. 'The wedding,' he said at last, 'was amazing. *The* event of the social year. Everyone who was anyone came. I was the pageboy who carried the ring.'

'You're kidding!' said Julie, stifling her mirth.

'Indeed I am not,' he said huffily. 'I was lovely then, at just seventeen. Small for my age. They said I looked younger. I could have been the next Nureyev, you know.'

Julie said nothing, let him ramble on. Once he had got it out of his system, she would bring on the heavier guns.

Ten years later their son was born. Esmée, by then, was in her late forties and the life she lived had not been conducive to conception.

'She was hardly ever at home,' he explained. 'The daughter was raised by the household staff. The Forresters were the king and queen of the stage. When the boy was born she went wild with delight. They named him Oberon to commemorate their first meeting.'

He described the occasion at Drury Lane when Esmée had brought the new baby onstage and held him aloft like a sporting trophy to the clamorous applause of the crowd.

'Another Forrester male is born,' she had proudly announced to the audience. 'To follow in his father's distinguished foot-steps.' Then, handing him to her beaming husband, she blew air kisses to the balcony. Somewhere, up in one of the boxes,

254

her ten-year-old daughter was looking on. In eight years' time she would be at RADA herself.

'Esmée always lived life to the full. It was one of the things her fans most enjoyed.' Beamish clearly had never been able to exorcise her ghost. 'For a week or so he went everywhere with her, as pampered as a lapdog. She enjoyed the role of devoted mother and hammed it up as much as she could. Until, one day, she realised how ageing it was. The baby was relegated to the wings and never again seen in public. Esmée reverted to playing the vamp. The world forgot she had children.'

'But what really happened? There has to be more.' Julie was growing impatient now. 'She can't just have given the whole thing up and vanished into thin air.'

'She died,' said Beamish, with misty eyes. 'At the absolute pinnacle of her fame. The papers all carried the story but then went silent.'

'Silent?'

'Silent. The world forgot. And five weeks later he was dead too, of cancer activated by a broken heart.'

'What happened?'

'An accident at home. She tripped on the stairs while arranging flowers and stabbed herself with her pruning shears.'

Even tough Julie recoiled at that. 'My God, what a horrible way to die! Surely they could have saved her? She was in her own home.'

Beamish said no. 'She was all alone. By the time she was found it was too late.' Crumpled at the foot of the stairs, the blade still stuck in her throat.

'But the children and the domestic staff?'

'Celeste was at RADA, in her second year. The boy saw it

happen but was only eight. There was nothing he could do to save her. He watched her bleed to death.'

'Wait a second,' cried Julie, disbelieving. 'He was old enough to have raised the alarm. He must have known about 999, could have simply run into the street for help. Eight is fully *compos mentis*, hardly a child any more.' The story simply didn't add up. Part of it must be missing.

'Ah,' said Beamish, suddenly sly. 'It wasn't quite that simple.'

43

It was days since he'd last had a full night's sleep; the Circle Line case was destroying his peace of mind. He couldn't stop thinking about Celeste and what he could do to exonerate her. Even though she refused to co-operate, he still had a feeling in his gut that she was holding something back, though he hadn't yet worked out what. He wondered if she was shielding some-one, which seemed the most likely scenario. Though what she hoped to achieve, he couldn't imagine. Again he drifted over to Tite Street and stood long minutes outside her house, remem-bering the night he had lingered there once before.

He stared up at the attic window where he had fancied he'd seen a light. Nothing there now but a blank façade with the curtains three-quarters closed. He rang the bell but nobody came, then stooped and peered through the letter box. All he could hear in the cavernous silence was the distant ticking of a clock. To gain admittance he would need a warrant but hadn't enough yet to justify that. Her face on film might place her in the store but not the murder weapon in her hand. They needed evidence to back it up: at the very least, a link between her and the victim. He could only hold her another two days, after which he was legally bound to let her go.

The simplest way forward would be if she'd learn to trust him.

She was pale and defiant yet beautiful when the warder ushered him into her cell. Whatever happens, don't screw this up, he prayed. The prison overall did her pasty skin and unwashed hair no favours, yet still she managed to stop the blood in his veins. He had never known anyone like her before. She rose from her seat on the hard narrow bed and received him like a society hostess without a hint of recognition. He had locked her up like an animal, thereby forfeiting any rights. She made it clear she resented this intrusion.

And yet they'd come close to falling in love, or so he sincerely believed. She had got to him in a way no other woman had. All his life he had trusted no one, especially since the booby trap, yet something about her defiant beauty touched the void in his heart. They were both emotionally crippled, it seemed. Not the best basis for love, perhaps, though he, at least, had been willing to give it a try.

Now here they were, in a prison cell, on opposite sides of the law. She facing charges of multiple murder; he there to put her inside if he could.

'Sorry to disturb you,' he said, indicating that she should sit. 'I've just looked in to check that you are all right.'

The ice in her eyes chilled him to the bone. 'Why are you really here?' she said. 'I have told you what little I know.'

'I need proof that you didn't commit this last murder. Remember, we have your face on film. Without some assistance from you, we can't let you go.'

'I wasn't even in the store,' she said. 'I have told you that several times. I was still travelling home at the time that woman was killed.'

'But in the vicinity of the store.'

'Along with several thousand others. Whoever the cameras caught, it wasn't me.'

Her indignation was so convincing, he almost believed she was telling the truth. But until she could prove she had not been there he had no other choice but to think her guilty. Which meant there could be no future in their friendship.

44

They caught the eight o'clock Eurostar, having met at Waterloo. Margaret had left at the crack of dawn to get there from Haywards Heath in time; Ellie was so fired up by the trip, she wanted to cram in as much as she possibly could. She was thrilled at the chance to see Paris after all. Wilbur, despite his parsimonious streak, always believed in pampering himself so had splurged on first-class tickets. Ellie and Margaret, excited as schoolgirls, faced each other in the exclusive seats and were instantly served with a glass of champagne before a lavish breakfast.

'This is certainly the life,' said Margaret, who at home would only have tea and toast. They had never travelled first class, especially after Jack retired. They had always looked for economy deals though had seen quite a lot of the world.

Ellie had never in her life before been to a country where she didn't know the language. She would not remotely have dared do it on her own. Their fellow travellers were businessmen, working on laptops or engrossed in the papers. The carriage had the feeling of a reading-room, and Ellie and Margaret lowered their voices, though could not prevent the occasional shriek of merriment bursting out. Poor old Wilbur, stuck in his bed. Ellie was sorry about the diagnosis although, if it led to his losing weight, it could only be for the best. All his life he had been a glutton and in recent years had been piling it on. She had given up trying to lecture him because he would not listen.

The waitress offered them more champagne, which both of them declined. They didn't want to be tipsy before they even got there.

He was just recovering from the shock when he spotted the card on the floor by the door. Julie Hudson of the *Daily Mail*. 'I would very much like to talk to you. If you would ring me at this number.' Brazen hussy; he cautiously checked but the street was now blessedly empty.

He was traumatised and began to shake. This was not something he'd handled before. Though Saturday nights saw his richest pickings, he cancelled his evening plans. They were closing in; he had seen it coming, though from another angle entirely. His sister's love life he could control. A national tabloid he could not. Sweating and scared, he withdrew to the cellar to pull another expensive cork and sit in the dark, away from prying eyes. His world was disintegrating all round. He might as well drink the lot.

Later, once he felt slightly calmer, his fighting spirit came surging back. There were very few people who had ever scared him; they did not include a sluttish girl. He knew it wasn't the long-haired one whose path he had tracked several times to the theatre. It must be the one with the spikes and short skirt. She had the look of a journalist. Well, Miss Hudson of the *Daily Mail*, now he knew where he could find her.

The hotel Wilbur had booked was small but beautifully situated, close to the Place Vendôme and the Tuileries gardens. Ellie suggested a second room but Margaret said she was happy to share. It was far more fun when travelling with a companion.

'If you're sure you don't mind.' Ellie was pleased. She was nervous of being alone in a foreign hotel. Suppose she needed to talk to the maid or ask for anything in the night? She wasn't used to travelling solo, was glad to have Margaret with her.

Despite the breakfast they'd had on the train, both were feeling peckish again so they dumped their bags and went straight out to get a feel of the city. It was Paris at its most alluring. The sun was high; their spirits too. They settled at an outside table and ordered two glasses of wine.

'*Vin ordinaire*. That's all right over here.' Margaret was still in charge of the drinks and Ellie more than content to let her order.

Margaret had been to Paris before, many times in her student years and fairly frequently ever since as she loved to browse in the galleries and museums. It was fun to be here with an ingénue who was wide-eyed with wonder at all the sights. Ellie made an enchanting companion, a mixture of girlish innocence and an insubordinate guile. Her observations made Margaret smile. She had clearly been married to Wilbur long enough. The demure appearance concealed an impressive intelligence.

She also knew a lot about art; Margaret was privately dazzled. She had, she explained, done an arts degree, though had never actually graduated since Wilbur had swept her off down the aisle before she had finished the course. In those days he had been very persuasive and, at least in her parents' eyes, quite a catch.

'The problem with Chippewa Falls,' she explained, 'is that it's stuck in a bit of a rut. Fine for baking pies and raising children but in no way intellectually stimulating.'

Here in Paris, with its bustling streets and all kinds of experiences waiting to be sampled, Ellie was finally coming into her own. London had been wonderful too but there she had been constrained by Wilbur. Margaret was an inspiring companion, energetic and knowledgeable, prepared to walk for miles without a murmur. Even the pavements, Ellie found, in Margaret's company seemed less hard. She was starting to open up like a Japanese flower.

Margaret admitted to being lonely; Ellie that her marriage was not up to scratch. Over quiet meals in cosy bistros, both let down their guards and poured out their hearts to each other. They ought never have moved from Croydon, said Margaret, but they hadn't known then that Jack would die. They had planned it as phase three of their lives, an exciting new beginning.

'He worked so hard, took so little time off, it seems unfair that he should have died so soon. He was a lovely man. I wish you had known him. I know he'd have taken to you.'

What would she do, Ellie wanted to know, to try to expand her horizons? Gardening, sewing cushion covers and babysitting for unappreciative children was not nearly enough for a woman not yet old with so many outside interests. Margaret laughed. She could not disagree. She had spent much time herself considering just that.

'Now that I've met you,' she confessed, 'I see what I mainly lack is a friend. Not just someone for shopping and coffee but a genuine kindred spirit.' Someone to go to the pictures with and discuss whatever might be troubling her. Someone to join her on cultural trips like this.

Ellie wholeheartedly agreed. She felt very much the same. This Paris trip had opened her eyes to what life untrammelled by a husband could be like. She had telephoned Wilbur several times and he'd grumbled a lot but patently did not miss her. The treatment was working, his blood sugar was down. They had it under control. He would be quite sorry to leave, he freely admitted.

'I hate to say it,' confided Ellie, 'but he's like an albatross round my neck. He has retired but I am more shackled than ever.' She had once suggested he iron his shirts and he'd looked at her in bewilderment. Household chores were a woman's domain. She had never once known him clear the dishes or even make himself a cup of coffee.

'He expects to be waited on hand and foot even though he has nothing much else to do. Slavery went out with Wilberforce but my Wilbur seems not to know that.'

They laughed, clasped hands and ordered a second bottle.

Margaret told her more about Jack and the cake he had iced one Christmas and Ellie said he'd deserved a medal for not being gender-bound.

'From all I've heard,' she said, 'you were very well matched.'

'We had a lot of interests in common. Liked walking and archaeological digs. When he retired we joined the National Trust.' She really should have kept up the visits but found it lonely doing things on her own. 'Next time you're over, perhaps you would join me on some outings.'

Ellie's regret, which she'd never told Wilbur, was having to give up her college degree. 'I'm not sure it would have made much difference but at least I'd have letters after my name and could maybe get a job in a museum.'

'You could do that now. It's never too late, not with adult education.' Margaret fancied training as a Blue Badge guide. It took two years and meant intensive study but would certainly get her out of the house and, indeed, enable her to meet new friends.

They finished their meal then, arm in arm, went off to see the Picasso museum, after which they planned to stroll along the Seine.

The actors' church in Covent Garden. It did make excellent sense. Imogen, whose heritage was the theatre, had thought of something that Julie had not. Of course that was where they'd be buried; she'd bet on it now. She left the office sharp at six, after making arrangements to meet colleagues later, and took the Underground to Covent Garden. It was still very hot; the Piazza was buzzing with street performers out in force. The first one who really caught her eye was a mime. He stood in one corner, not on a box but on his own like a marionette with his sad, white-painted face. He drooped, like Chaplin beneath a lamp-post, waiting for someone to work his strings and when Julie stopped, amused, to admire him, he rolled his heavily made-up eyes and gave her all he'd got. She loved it. He was the real thing, as Marcel Marceau as they came, by far the best she had ever seen in London. If he'd had a cap, which he didn't, which seemed odd, she would have made a donation.

She found the church with no trouble at all, right in the middle of theatreland, a masterpiece by the architect Inigo Jones.

Inside it was spacious and filled with light as the setting sun cast its rays through the glorious windows. Julie moved slowly down each aisle, carefully reading each wall-mounted plaque, anxious not to miss a single one. She found Vivien Leigh and Edith Evans and a host of other illustrious names. Now that she knew that the daughter was living she had very strong hopes she would find the son. Rupert should be pleased with her. She felt she might be close to winning the jackpot.

45

The mime was there when she left the church, having found what she had been looking for, only this time he had moved considerably closer. He showed no sign of being alive, was slumped, hands in pockets, against a railing, his deadpan face with its great tragic eyes focused blankly into space. Beneath each eye he had painted a teardrop and his scarlet mouth drooped in abject despair. He wore a red-striped matelot shirt, black pants and neat white gloves. His hair was covered by a curly wig, traditional in the old-fashioned way. Perhaps he was performing somewhere nearby.

She was meeting colleagues for supper at Orso's so made her way slowly across the Piazza, still thronging with tourists and workers on their way home. Imogen's hunch had turned out to be right. Both the Forresters were buried there, though their plaque simply gave the briefest of details with no mention of progeny. Still, it was a start: the dates were there. They had died, as Beamish had said, within weeks of each other. So what had happened to their son if the daughter still lived in the house? Julie felt really fired by the progress she'd made.

One of her colleagues from the paper was moving on to higher things. A bunch of them were throwing an impromptu party. There were twelve of them seated round one table and the noise they made was stupendous. The other diners at this hour were mainly headed to the theatre and appeared not to mind. Julie was wearing her shortest skirt and highest heels for the occasion. The two other women in the party left early. Julie could drink as well as the blokes and the wine was certainly flowing that night. The management brought replacements as fast as they could. It was gone eleven by the time they dispersed, so Julie headed to Leicester Square to catch the tube to Notting Hill.

He was there again as she crossed the Piazza, this time juggling balls. A small crowd stood around him, cheering him on. Julie liked his doleful face, which never seemed to alter its expression. She wondered what it would take to get him to smile. This time he did have his cap on the ground so she tossed him a couple of pounds as she passed; she hoped she would see him again.

There were acrobats performing nearby and a Creole jazz band playing in Jubilee Market. It was Tuesday night; the place was jumping even as late as this. The hot summer's night was fragrant with incense and the candyfloss smell of cheap tobacco. Julie loitered, enjoying the ambience, and on an impulse stopped for another drink. This was the city she'd adopted when she'd managed to make the break from the north. As soon as she could afford the rent, she hoped to move into Soho. She sat outside with her glass of wine and tapped her foot to the lively music. She was thrilled with where she had got with her research. First thing tomorrow she would talk to Rupert. She hoped he would let her help with the book. This could well be the big step forward she needed.

It was time to go or she'd miss her train. The fastest route was down Maiden Lane. The crowds were thinner there and it was darker. A figure stepped suddenly out of the shadows, the white-faced mime, still wearing his gloves, his face fixed into a tragic mask, accentuated by the painted teardrops. Julie, startled, stopped dead in her tracks. For a second he'd really scared her.

'Hello!' she said, once she'd caught her breath. This surely had to be more than coincidence. She wondered if he had followed her. Unless, of course, he was a different mime.

He didn't respond to her friendly greeting, just stood there, blocking her progress in the narrow lane. Then slowly he started to back away, beckoning her with one white-gloved finger until he vanished round the corner into an unlit courtyard. Julie laughed, enjoying the game, which was doubtless part of his act. He was probably a student from drama school earning money in the vacation. Soon he'd unmask and they'd have a good laugh, might even manage another drink if she caught the night bus home.

There was a restaurant across the courtyard with bursts of laughter from within. The whole world seemed to be partying tonight. Julie went with the flow. Laughing herself, she followed him, away from the lighted street and into the shadows. What a lark. She would tell the girls and they must come here again another evening.

*   *   *

Just for a moment she thought she'd lost him till a lamp picked out his white face. He was standing silently waiting for her in the corner.

'Hang on, I'm coming,' called Julie gaily, tripping across the cobbles on her high heels. This was turning into quite an adventure, a filler for the paper maybe. A touch of authentic Dickensian London for the readers. There was obvious movement inside the restaurant, which must be heading for closing time. Soon the diners would issue forth and the moment would be lost. She moved up close and touched his arm to let him know she was there.

For a long rapt moment he stared at her and she stared back at his dead-white face. Even this close she could not make out exactly what he looked like. His hair was concealed beneath the wig; his hands by the tight white gloves. He stood with a dancer's rigid pose, his feet in their black ballet shoes turned out. There were big dark circles round his eyes and tiny comma-like eyebrows. It must take him hours to apply all that paint. She wondered if he went home like that or had somewhere he could change. His mouth was fixed in a downward arc. She had a sudden desire to make him smile.

She trusted him instinctively; he was part of the night theatre. So when he beckoned again she obediently followed. Into the shadows, away from the lamp; she wondered if he'd reveal himself, whether perhaps he was someone she knew simply having a laugh. She moved a bit closer, flirtatiously, prepared for whatever he had to offer. But still he beckoned and, what the hell, there were plenty of people about.

Just for a moment she thought he would kiss her until the light glinted off the knife and she knew, too late, she had badly misjudged him. Then he laughed, oh how he laughed, as the blade went in and she crumpled at his feet. He stood there silently guffawing and the garish arc reversed itself. The mournful eyes now revealed their dislike. He stepped over her body in his ballet shoes and faded into the night.

46

Detective Inspector Brewster arrived in a big official car though, to both girls' surprise, was wearing plainclothes. He stopped in the doorway and patted the dogs, who bounced around him with waving tails and none of the fake aggression they sometimes showed.

'What lovely animals.' His smile was broad, his handshake agreeably firm. Though he walked with an almost imperceptible limp, both of them found him very attractive despite the scar on his face.

Imogen led him to the drawing room, having shut the dogs in the kitchen, out of the way. Brewster seated himself in an armchair and the girls perched side by side on a couch. They were both so young, he thought, and so vulnerable. It sickened his heart that these things should occur. Life in London grew daily grimmer. He looked around and admired the room, then courteously asked them about themselves. Was gravely impressed that Alice sold books and that Imogen was a dancer.

'I will certainly come to your show,' he said. He might even invite Celeste. It was early days, he was well aware, and they both had a lot of bridges to mend but he still had hopes that they might make it once she was cleared of suspicion. He would have to release her now, knowing she could not have been implicated in Julie's death, though she still had a lot of explaining to do, not least how her face had been caught on camera when she swore that she hadn't been in the store. This, however, was far more urgent. He would sort things out with Celeste when he had the time.

After some more congenial chat, he pulled out his notebook and turned to Alice.

'You shared a flat, I understand, with the victim, Julie Hudson.'

Alice nodded and gave him the details. He could see how shattered she was. When the squad car had arrived in the middle of the night, neither of them could believe the news, even though Julie was out a lot and occasionally drank too much. The police had gone first to Onslow Gardens and the downstairs neighbour had directed them here.

Brewster asked how she'd first met Julie. Alice told him about the typing course.

'So you must have known her well,' he said. 'Was she, perhaps, your closest friend?'

No, that was Imogen, Alice explained, which was how she came to be living here while Imogen's parents were away in France. All she and Julie had been was flatmates, though of course she'd been very fond of her and was horrified by her death.

'And did you spend much of your time together? Apart from living beneath one roof.'

'Quite a lot,' said Alice, considering. 'We ate at home maybe once a week and hung around together at weekends.'

'So you knew each other's friends,' he suggested, scribbling her answers in his notebook.

'Not really,' said Alice. They had moved in quite different circles. The only ones she had met were men, usually connected with her work. The *Daily Mail*, she told him, which Brewster knew.

Something about him warmed Imogen's heart, even now when she was so shaken. He gave the impression of strength and stability, both qualities she admired in Duncan. No wonder her mother had married him. Men like that were quite rare these days. Knowing Brewster was on the case made Imogen feel far less threatened. Her mother was insisting on coming straight home although she had begged her not to. She had Alice here as well as the dogs. And now they had this policeman.

Brewster was thinking how cute they were; bright and gutsy and brave. Despite the horror of their close friend's death, they appeared to be coping remarkably well. He was glad the parents were coming home. It was just conceivable these girls might be targets too. He leafed through his notes while he thought about it; when Imogen offered him coffee, he gladly accepted. The murder, he'd guess, was most likely random, a pretty girl on her own late at night, lured into a dark cul-de-sac and knifed.

But you never knew. This latest attack bore all the hallmarks of the Circle Line killer. The vicious stabbing, the blood, the screams, close to a street that was thronging with life, just yards away from a packed and popular restaurant. The murderer must have nerves of steel and seemed to be making a show of it. Either he was growing careless or else he wanted to be caught.

Imogen could add very little. She hadn't really known Julie well though had lately started to like her a lot, had been helping her with some research. She began to cry; it was hard to take in even now, after more than twenty-four hours. Alice leaned over and touched her hand; they were clearly very close. Brewster was glad they had each other. After he'd been through the rig-marole, the routine questions that had to be asked and might possibly lead to something, he closed his notebook and settled back. You learnt more, he'd found, from informal chat. He had been in this game a long time now and knew which buttons to press

Imogen brought the coffee in and the dogs came thundering back. They slavered and wagged but were well behaved. At a word from her, they crouched down. It was excellent that she had them here, both as company and protection. Brewster had checked and the house seemed commendably secure.

'Right,' he said, when he took his leave. 'I want you both to promise me one thing.' He handed each of them his business card. 'This is my direct line,' he said. 'Call me any time, night or day, if you think of anything or feel scared. I promise you I'll pick up.'

'Thanks,' said Imogen, showing him out. 'But you don't have to worry. We've got the dogs.'

As if they'd be any protection at all against a madman with a knife.

47

'We have to go home,' said Beth in France. 'We can't possibly leave them alone without any protection.' Duncan was on to the ferry company but apparently not making very much progress. There was some sort of strike that they couldn't explain; his French was still far short of the local patois. He hadn't even got Richard to translate since he'd gone to Toulouse to see the picture framer.

'They are both grown up.' Duncan did have a point. Plus the dogs would look after them. He had absolute faith in his Weimaraners who were tougher than they seemed. Right now his priority was his wife who had worked all summer without a break and had been through that ghastly experience with the bombs. He couldn't have borne anything happening to her. Although they had now been together ten years, she remained the focus of his life. 'They can come out here when they get the

OK.' A detective was seeing them both that day. 'Richard has said all along that everyone's welcome.'

Beth mulled it over then talked to Jane who had been there for several days. 'Will you think me a bad mother if I don't go home?'

'I can't really see why they need you there. Duncan is right: they're no longer kids. They are both professionals, with jobs to do, who may even cope better on their own.'

So it was settled. Jane usually won since she brought a new perspective to things. Duncan stopped trying to book the ferry, promising Beth that, if need be, he would fly her home in a couple of hours instead of going by car.

Imogen felt she was being watched as she left for the theatre that afternoon. She shrugged it off as part of the trauma caused by Julie's murder. The Circle Line was running again. She was determined to chance it. Alice was also back at work: there was no point hanging around in the house. It might help her come to terms with it all if she had something to do.

'Feel free to call if you need to talk,' she had said before leaving for the shop. She normally didn't like personal calls while she was serving customers but these were unusual circumstances; they badly needed to support each other. The thought of returning to Onslow Gardens filled Alice with utter revulsion. Both, however, were level-headed. Some blame must surely attach to Julie for staying out late and having too much to drink.

Imogen had walked the dogs then carefully shut them in the kitchen, Alice would let them out when she got home. Her mother had rung a couple more times, to check that things were still all right. Duncan was taking them out to lunch while

Richard was back in his studio, working. It sounded normal and very relaxed. The last thing Imogen wanted to do was get her fretting again.

But she still had that feeling, kept glancing round in case there was someone following her, but all she saw was a mass of people going about their business. In the Tube she found she couldn't concentrate, kept checking to see who got on and off, though no one seemed to be taking much notice of her. At this time of day, in the late afternoon, the carriages were relatively empty. She would be at the theatre by the time the real rush hour began.

Hungerford Bridge, though, was already busy. There were more pedestrians on the bridge than traffic on the road. Imogen pushed her way through the crowd, anxious to be at the theatre on time, still with that eerie sensation of being watched. Her mother had jokingly warned her about this. The star syndrome, she called it. Once you have made it, it never lets up; you can no longer call your life your own. The fact she was only in the chorus appeared not to register with Beth. Imogen felt inconspicuous yet the eerie feeling persisted.

After the show she experienced it again, though the South Bank was pulsating. She paused on the steps and looked around. People were strolling along the river on their way home from an evening out. The audience from the Festival Hall mingled with that of the National Theatre to make it doubly busy.

Very close to where she stood, a small crowd was grouped around a mime, laughing and applauding his various poses. Dressed in black with a red and white T-shirt, he battled against an invisible wind, then was dragged along by a forceful dog, his face a mask of desperate bewilderment. Imogen wandered over to watch, forgetting, at least for a moment, her preoccupation. The mime was better than the living statues; at least he displayed real skill. He wore thick white make-up, with painted teardrops beneath each black-circled eye, mournful and staring like a crazed raccoon, and small surprised eyebrows like commas. He wrestled with imaginary balloons as if they were going to carry him off. Imogen chuckled and clapped very hard. He was good.

In lighter spirits she set off home, over the bridge where the crowd had now thinned, towards the welcoming lights of Embankment station. Thoughts of Julie and her terrible death still weighed heavily on her mind. If only she hadn't gone drinking that night on her own.

Alice should have been home some time, waiting up for her with the dogs. They would eat late supper and catch up on each other's day. Imogen loved having Alice to stay. Apart from being her childhood friend, Alice was someone to whom she could talk openly about these paranoid fears. Her mother would only have made a fuss and stopped her travelling on the Circle Line, but Imogen felt it was nothing much more than the shock of a close friend's death.

Halfway across the bridge she stopped and had another quick look round. Right at the end, from where she had come, a slight black figure was advancing fast, carrying something bulky in his hand. Everyone else was in couples or groups. Only Imogen seemed to be on her own.

You are being neurotic, she told herself, then impulsively pulled out her phone and punched out Brewster's number.

Just as he'd said, he answered at once.

'I'm probably just being silly,' she said. 'But I have a persistent feeling of being followed.'

'Just keep on coming,' said Brewster calmly, 'and try not to lose your nerve. Don't look round or attempt to confront him. Whoever it is may be dangerous. Move quickly but don't draw attention to yourself. We'll be waiting for you at the station.'

48

It seemed as though he came out of nowhere, from the darkness of the railway arches alongside the entrance to the Underground station. She didn't immediately know who he was, a tall man in an anonymous raincoat, wearing dark glasses even at this time of night. He gripped her elbow, which was how she knew it was him.

'You startled me,' she said, alarmed, instinctively backing away. She had spent the whole day in a nervous state. This cloak and dagger stuff did not improve things.

'Sorry,' said Brewster, 'if I startled you. But we think we may have a possible lead. It's vital that we should not be seen together.' He drew her stealthily into the shadows. 'Tell me precisely what you think you saw. Have you any idea who it might have been? Perhaps an acquaintance of Julie's?'

Imogen ruefully rubbed her arm where his fingers had gripped her too hard. Detective Inspector Brewster seemed unusually tense.

'It was nothing really,' she tried to explain, regretting now having made the call, sure that he must think her a total fool. 'It was just that I have the weirdest sensation that someone is constantly watching me. And you did say we should call you at any time.'

She looked around for Brewster's partner, knowing they usually worked in pairs.

'He's over there,' he said, understanding at once. 'Keeping an eye on the exit.'

He led her further into the gloom, which hardly improved the state of her nerves. She knew very little about this man except that he had appeared when Julie was killed. On that occasion, she now recalled, he had not worn uniform either.

She edged away. 'It's all right,' she said. The station was teeming with late-night travellers. 'I can manage now. Thanks for coming so quickly. I am truly sorry if I've wasted your time.'

'Look,' said Brewster, grabbing her again. 'We are here entirely for your protection. This isn't a game. There's a killer at large and, until he's caught, you are none of you safe. Keep your eyes peeled and call me whenever you need to. I can't overemphasise the importance of that.'

'Why me?' asked Imogen, startled and shocked.

'Partly because you were Julie's friend. And also because . . . well, you fit the general description.'

'Description of what?' Now she really was scared.

'Of his other victims.' He'd have thought she'd have known. He offered to see her on to the train but Imogen laughed in his face.

I am not a child, she almost said but could see he was far from being amused. And she had been scared, she couldn't

286

overlook that. Julie had died. It was good of them to come. If someone was on a killing spree she didn't want to end up one of his victims.

Alice was in the kitchen reading, the dogs lying peacefully at her feet. She'd adapted easily to Chepstow Villas, but then it was almost her second home since she had spent so much time there in her youth. There was something delicious keeping warm in the Aga; the smell of it was divine. She had even deferred having supper herself until Imogen got home.

'I saw the cop again tonight,' said Imogen, opening a bottle of Chablis. 'I called him and he met me at the station.'

'Why?' asked Alice, instantly anxious. She hated Imogen being out late every night.

'I got scared,' said Imogen, 'crossing the bridge. I had the sensation of being followed.' Eyes upon her was how it had felt, though, in such a crowd, how could she possibly tell? 'I'm sure it was just an emotional reaction in the aftermath of Julie's death. I look for murderers everywhere now, though don't know how I would recognise one. I doubt they look any different from you or me.'

'Thanks,' said Alice, tasting the wine and nodding her head in approval. She knew precisely what Imogen meant, had felt spooked herself when she got on the Tube.

She carried the casserole to the table while Imogen got out the plates. Unlike Imogen, Alice was perfectly house-trained. Imogen sniffed with appreciation. Home felt good, especially with Alice here. The house was spacious, with plenty of rooms, yet the kitchen had always been its heart. Even without the presence of Beth, she could wrap it round her like a chinchilla scarf. The dogs, the Aga, the tick of the clock, the ingrained aromas of legendary meals all contributed to its aura of complete domestic calm. Here, not only because of the dogs, she always felt totally safe.

'Your mother rang to see how things were. I told her there was no need for alarm. I think I finally convinced her that she needn't hurry home.'

There she went, scurrying across the bridge, the flibbertigibbet with the streaming hair and a face that was almost as beautiful as his own. He let her go, was in no special hurry; enjoyed this new game of cat and mouse. He knew where to look for her; there was no great hurry. He leaned on the parapet, gazing down at the river. One simple dive was all it would take to find the blessed release he had endlessly yearned for. He had felt that faint urge throughout his life but lately things had subtly started to change. He'd experienced a thrill he had never imagined when he'd shoved that unknown commuter under a train.

The thrill of killing had made him mature. He was no longer the boy who was hidden away. Since he'd started roaming the streets at night and doing his thing on the Underground he had suddenly found his place in life, his fulfilment. At first he'd selected them randomly, from the sheer frustration of seeing them happy, watching them laughing into their phones, regardless of those around them. The second one, which they had realised was murder because of the knife jutting out of her back, had started a brouhaha in the press that had got him really fired up. Too long had he been anonymous, deprived of the platform that was his by right, the child of performers he longed to emulate.

All those evenings spent sitting on the stairs, invisible to the glittering crowd, watching his parents entertain and his sister showing off. How he had longed to be one of them, to take his natural place at their side. To become the star he had always known was his birthright. But now he had found his natural bent, life was beginning to be worth living. He could choose them now and take his time. With each one he killed he felt a growing catharsis.

He had finished his business for the night. Now it was time to go home. To an empty house with nobody there, where he could do as he damn well pleased, eat his meals in the dining room, get drunk in his father's cellar. Mount the stairs knowing she wouldn't be there, use the key he ought not to have and let himself into the paradise of his mother's inherited things. He had worshipped her from an early age, yet she had cast him aside. Too busy to learn to communicate; too arrogant to accept she'd been wrong. He was only allowed in her presence as a concession.

He had been there the day of the accident, had sat and watched her bleed slowly to death. Had seen she was mouthing something though didn't know what. Afterwards he had stroked her hands, had arranged her skirts as they should have been. Had brushed her hair and restored it to its coiffure. She had looked so helpless, like a broken doll, while he, for the first time ever, felt fully alive.

The sight of her lying there on the stairs, her hair all loose and soaked in her blood, had released an image in his brain he endlessly tried to perpetuate. Death was good. It had caught her in her full glory.

49

They had let her go, he had seen to that, on the condition that she made no attempt to leave town. She was off the hook but only just. Numerous questions remained that would require answers. Especially how she'd been caught on closed-circuit TV. He was out there waiting when she emerged, standing beside the official car with only the driver and one uniformed officer to accompany them on the ride. She was pale yet still very much in control. He held the door open while she got in, then took his seat beside her. He suspected she'd sooner have gone by taxi but today that was not an option. They rode in silence. It was late afternoon. The sky was still bright though the sun would shortly be setting.

She stared abstractedly out of the window as though hungry for her freedom. It was four days since they had taken her in, and she wore the same clothes that she'd worn then. In the interim she had been in prison garb.

After a while, he broke the silence, unable to stand the atmosphere any longer.

'Will there be anyone waiting at home? A family member, perhaps?'

She hesitated then shook her head. She had left so abruptly in the early hours, snatched from her bed like a criminal, that no one knew except her employer who was loyally standing by her. They reached the house, which appeared shut up. Brewster recalled the flicker of light he had seen.

'Would you like me to come in with you?'

She thought for a second then shook her head. But he felt instinctively that she was gradually thawing. When he asked if he might see her later, she said yes.

'Come back in a couple of hours,' she said. 'Give me time to freshen up.' She suddenly smiled. 'I am not about to jump bail.'

'Take as long as you like,' he said. 'I'll meet you at eight in the restaurant on the corner.'

In Cannon Street he reviewed the case. It very much looked as though they were back to square one. If she wasn't guilty, and he now believed it, then a dangerous killer was still at large and he had no answer to the burning question of how she'd been caught by the cameras. It was only her word, he could not overlook that, yet instinct told him she was telling the truth. He planned to use the kid glove treatment in order to get her to talk.

They met in the local bistro at eight. She had washed her hair and changed her clothes and generally cleaned herself up. The smile she gave him seemed genuine.

'How are things at home?' he asked.

'Everything's under control.' She seemed warmer now and

292

more relaxed away from the grimness of that prison cell. As well she might; she was free again, or would be when she'd given him satisfactory answers.

'This has to be off the record,' he said. 'But, without prejudice, I believe in your innocence. I will do all I can to get you off but only if you are honest with me. I like you too much to watch you rot in jail.'

At that she grinned and her eyes lit up. At last it appeared he might be making headway.

The menu came but Celeste couldn't eat. She was far too strung up for that. She knew she was going to have to confide in him; there was no other way. He ordered oysters and steak tartare with a fine red wine to accompany it.

'You must build yourself up,' he told her with a smile.

He waited until she appeared relaxed, then started in with the questions. He could only help her, he said again, if she would learn to trust him. She fidgeted with her oyster fork while she struggled with a decision. Then raised her luminous eyes to his and started to fill him in on the missing pieces. He was, she explained, her younger brother, the only family she had left. Then she told him the whole wretched story, starting nine months before his birth with her mother's bout of German measles which had effectively ruined his life.

As a child he had been endearingly sweet, with a trusting nature and a gentle spirit. She had cherished and protected him and, for a while, it had worked. His mother's death had traumatised him; he had seen her fall, unable to help in any way. Celeste had come home in the late afternoon and found him still sitting on the stairs, with Esmée all covered in blood, her throat slashed open. At first she thought she had broken her neck until she had seen the pruning shears. Flowers had been one of her mother's passions; she liked to arrange them herself.

They had managed to cover the whole thing up. The press only knew she had fallen. But her father had guessed the truth and could not forgive him. He had issued a statement. The case was closed. The child was sent to an institution where he'd stayed until she turned twenty-one and became his legal guardian. The deal was he had to stay under her care, but then there was nowhere else he could go.

Five weeks after Esmée's death, Sir Edward died too of virulent cancer, accelerated, it was said, by a broken heart. Celeste was left with a shattered future and a pile of debts she worked hard to pay off. Most of this she related to Brewster though not the most crucial part. When he asked her where her brother was now, she told him she didn't know.

'So was it your brother in Peter Jones?' He had noted the slightly androgynous look of the slim dark figure they'd seen racing up the stairs.

'Perhaps. We do look rather alike and he has always had a thing about dressing up – a throwback to our mother.'

He had always been mad. She saw that now. Driven to it by his stunted childhood and a tragic twist of fate.

'What am I going to do?' she asked.

'Leave it to us,' said Brewster.

It was after midnight; the street was deserted. He groped for his key when he turned the corner then stopped abruptly in his tracks. The house, which was usually shrouded in darkness, tonight was a blaze of light. His heart started beating wildly with shock. It seemed his fortifications had been breached. The drawing-room chandeliers were ablaze as well as the lights on the staircase. Someone was in there ahead of him. He could only hope it was her.

She was standing at the top of the stairs, the moon back-lighting her like an apparition, wearing one of her mother's diaphanous gowns. She held a heavy silver candlestick in case, perhaps, he might be an intruder. He dropped his bag and peeled off the wig, unwrapping the scarf from round his face, revealing the garish make-up. He was glad and relieved that she was there. He relied upon her completely. His face broke into the smile that was so like hers.

'They are on to you,' was all she said. 'If I were you I'd get out of here before they bring a warrant for your arrest.' There was genuine pity on her face as she turned and went into her room.

Wait, he wanted to say to her, making a lunge towards her door. But when he tried it, he found it already locked.

50

The Paris trip seemed to hurtle by, and before they knew it they were back on the train, agreeing to do it again some time, circumstances permitting. They had worked the city until they dropped, seen all the galleries and museums, even been up the Eiffel Tower and shopped in the Champs Elysées.

'I am really going to miss you,' said Margaret.

'Me too,' said Ellie glumly.

Tomorrow Wilbur would be discharged and they'd fly straight home to Chippewa Falls. She looked forward to seeing her grandchildren again but not to very much else. It would mean returning to the old routines, with Wilbur under her feet even more since he wouldn't be playing golf again for a while.

'I expect the baby has grown,' she said before falling into a grave and thoughtful silence.

Margaret attempted to cheer her up but was feeling equally glum. They had had such good times and really clicked. It seemed a pity they lived so far apart. They were served an elegant three-course meal with an interesting choice of French wines. Ellie began to brighten up; the sparkle returned to her eyes. They chatted a bit about what they'd seen, in particular the Picasso museum in its seventeenth-century house.

'I would have liked more time there,' said Ellie. 'There was too much to see in one visit.'

She reminisced about her arts course, the painters she had studied. Margaret's plan to train as a guide had activated an idea in her head. 'If I lived in London what I'd most like to do is work at the V&A.'

She fell silent again for a while until, outside Lille, she had her epiphany. With heightened colour and a tightened jaw she sat bolt upright in her seat, looked at Margaret fair and square and said: 'I am not going back.'

'What?' said Margaret, who was reading the guidebook, having not quite taken in what Ellie had said.

'I am going to tell Wilbur I am not going home, that I'm staying on in London. He has had the best years of my life, though never appreciated the fact. Now he can learn to look after himself. I am quitting.'

'You're crazy,' said Margaret, but Ellie's mood was infectious. They ordered brandies and toasted her resolution.

Wilbur was waiting when Ellie arrived, bringing him his street clothes. He paid the bill with a credit card and shook the matron by the hand. No hint of a present but that was Wilbur. Ellie did the honours with chocolates and flowers. They had done a wonderful job for him; he was able to walk with a couple of sticks. He would only need them until he'd recovered his balance. The nurses stood and waved him off as Ellie assisted him into the cab. The moment they'd turned the corner, he started complaining.

He had hated the food, the bed was hard and at night he had found it difficult to sleep because they kept the lights on. They had given him pills to knock him out then woken him at a ridiculous hour to ask if he needed a bedpan and give him more pills. They had not approved of his poker games because it impeded the hospital's daily routines. He was putting this matter into the hands of his lawyers.

Yes, thought Ellie, but they'd taken him in and seemed to have worked an extraordinary cure. Not only was he able to walk but he had dropped ten pounds in weight. They had put him on a special diet, excluding most of the things he liked but pointing the way to a much more healthy future. And, as Margaret had pointed out, they were only charging him for the bed. All the medical treatment came free, courtesy of the NHS which Ellie knew was grotesquely overworked. But there was no point trying to point this out. Besides, she was long past caring.

They ate an indifferent dinner in the dismal hotel. The dining room was crowded with yet more tourists. Ellie sat silent while Wilbur talked, pontificating about the food, the weather, the traffic noises and the hefty bill. They wouldn't be staying here again. He was going to complain to the travel firm. Ellie reflected how kind Tom had been but still didn't utter a word.

Back in their room, as they started to pack, she announced that she was leaving him. She had thought about it long and hard and would not reverse the decision. To start with, he didn't take in what she'd said, was preoccupied with the snooker game on TV. But when her words finally did sink in, he simply dismissed them with an incredulous laugh.

'What are you going to live on?' he asked when at last he saw that she really meant it. He had been through her Paris expenses in detail and queried every small bill.

'On half of what you are worth,' she said. 'Unless you let the whole matter drop. In which case I'll settle for my living expenses to keep me afloat while I look for a job. After which I don't need a thing from you. I intend to stand on my own feet.'

After Wilbur had left for the airport, spluttering yet unwilling to risk missing his flight, Ellie phoned Margaret to tell her how it had gone.

'I did it,' she said, 'and he took it badly. Is still recovering from the shock. I have hung on to the traveller's cheques which should keep me afloat for a while.'

Margaret was shattered but also amused. There was far more to Ellie than met the eye. 'How are you going to live?' she wanted to know.

'I'm not entirely destitute. Though he believes I am. I have got a few paintings at home that are worth quite a lot. He thinks I'll be back in a couple of weeks, unable to hack it on my own. But he's mistaken. I've never felt better in my life.'

Lovely Tom, who had been so kind, would help her find a cheap room somewhere until she had fully worked out her future alone.

'You know you can come and stay with me.' Margaret was secretly overjoyed.

'I was rather relying on your saying that,' said Ellie.

51

It was Saturday night and a sell-out show. Only two weeks to the end of the run and tickets for *Anything Goes* were now like gold dust. Lots of people who were really big time were due backstage to pay their respects and celebrate a truly outstanding production. There was talk of renewals and fat new contracts, as well as a transfer to Broadway next year. Imogen knew that she had to stay on, even though she felt nervous of travelling home so late. Duncan would have told her to take a taxi, since he couldn't be there to pick her up, but in that vicinity at that hour taxis were even harder to come by than tickets.

Tonight, unusually, she was dressed to the nines. Normally she changed into sweat pants after the show. But Alice insisted she must look her best, since the paparazzi would be there in droves and the moguls that mattered present. She had borrowed sandals from another dancer, in which she could scarcely walk, just a couple of diamanté straps with higher heels than she'd ever dared try before. The dress she had bought for the occasion was so low cut that it felt obscene. She had searched through her mother's closet for a pashmina.

'It's important you look the part,' said Alice, uncharacteristically clued up. 'If you are going to make it to the top.'

The mime was there, right outside the theatre. Imogen passed him as she went in. Doing his act with the balloons and the dog. She stopped for two minutes to cheer him on, thinking of him as a kind of good-luck charm. Something about his droll appearance got to her and cheered her up. On impulse, she dropped a fiver in his cap, certain he must be aware of her. It was hard to know from that deadpan face, but struggling thespians should always be there for each other.

Now here she was, at a quarter to twelve, full of champagne and on top of the world, urgently needing to leave to catch that last train. Originally Alice had wanted to come but had had to cry off as her brother was getting engaged. Besides, she'd already seen the show several times. Normally Beth and Duncan would be there, but they were still in France.

She said her good nights, then slipped away, as if to a waiting limousine. The dress and the heels were not quite the thing for crossing the bridge late at night. A powerful breeze was coming off the river. It felt as though there might be a storm; she noticed in passing that the mime had gone. Although there was virtually no one about, she couldn't shake off the feeling of being followed.

Embankment station was almost deserted. She caught the train by the skin of her teeth, slowed down by the unaccustomed height of her heels. Alone in the carriage, she finally relaxed. Only eight stations to Notting Hill Gate, followed by a two-minute hobble to the house. She had nothing planned for the following day and could do with a long lie-in. In the afternoon she would take the dogs to the park.

A couple got in at Westminster then off again at Victoria. Imogen, feeling slightly squiffy, closed her eyes. The train pulled out of the station then stopped. Its engine shuddered, gave a kind of sigh, then died. She opened her eyes in sudden alarm, caught a glimpse of a figure at the end of the carriage that definitely hadn't been there before, and then the lights went out. There was absolute silence apart from her heartbeat, hammering frantically in her chest. She strained her ears for sounds of movement but couldn't hear anything at all. Petrified, she grabbed her phone, and, as she was searching for Brewster's number, the lights came on again.

In the darkness, he had moved closer to her, a black-clad figure with a chalk-white face, and was standing motionless, drooping from a strap, staring at her with melancholy eyes. Imogen felt almost faint with relief; it was only her friend, the mime. He wore the same outfit, the candy-striped T-shirt under a clinging black one-piece jumpsuit, and his painted mouth turned down in mock despair. Imogen smiled and greeted him but he neither said a word nor moved a muscle.

There was something creepy about him now, just hanging there like a marionette with nobody working its strings. She had given him quite a hefty tip; surely he must remember her. Could that conceivably be why he was here? It seemed absurd to remain in character with an audience of only one. She pulled her mother's pashmina closer and smiled again but he still didn't move. By now she was starting to find him faintly disturbing.

She rose to her feet and edged away, wishing she wasn't wearing the sandals, then moved to the end of the carriage, phone in hand. Brewster's number was still lit up. She punched it in then turned back to face the mime, who'd advanced several yards and also altered his pose.

Brewster answered on the second ring. She was badly shaken by now. What had seemed a joke was starting to be very frightening. She was stuck in a tunnel with a crazy person who refused to speak or acknowledge her. If the lights went out again, she would die of fright.

'I am on the train,' she virtually whispered, turning her back so the mime couldn't hear. At which point the engine growled back into life and the train inched slowly forward. 'Just beyond Victoria station.' He had somehow managed to come even closer without her seeing him move. 'I am on my own and there's someone who's starting to scare me.'

'Listen very carefully,' said Brewster calmly, not even sounding surprised. 'We are waiting for you at Sloane Square station. The train's almost here; I can see its lights. Try to stay calm, just get off quickly and take the escalator up to the street. Don't worry. We'll have you covered. There is nothing to fear.'

The lights of the station were now in sight; Imogen moved to the door. The mime still hung there, not moving a muscle except that his painted mouth had reversed into a terrifying grin.

Because she had only just caught the train, leaping into the very last carriage, she now was faced with the length of the platform before she could reach the exit. She stumbled slightly on the stupid heels, glancing around her for signs of life, aware that the mime was right behind her, gaining rapidly on her in his ballet shoes. Where was Brewster? He'd promised to be here. Her heart was in her mouth.

'Stop!' a voice ordered through a megaphone, and there he was, in uniform this time, accompanied by a fierce-looking dog wearing a yellow flak jacket.

'Run,' Brewster told her, 'and don't look back. Just get yourself up to the street. The rest of the squad is waiting there. You have nothing to worry about now.'

Imogen took her sandals off and ran like a deer on her dancer's feet, along the platform and, in one graceful leap, on to the escalator.

She didn't know what was happening behind her. All she could think about was not getting killed.

Brewster and Burgess watched the train pull out and Imogen running for all she was worth, followed on silent feet by the weird-looking mime. The empty platform stretched before her but, boy, how that girl could move. He was fast but she was faster. Brewster remembered the one in the veil, who could never have stood a chance.

He raised his megaphone again. 'Stop!' he ordered. 'Or else I'll shoot.' There were armed policeman waiting outside, as well as Celeste, who'd been brought along for formal identification. The mime never faltered, just continued to sprint, pacing Imogen like a predatory beast even though she was now on the escalator and he couldn't possibly catch her.

The dog was straining so hard on the leash that his front paws were off the ground.

'Go get him, Burgess!' said Brewster, raising his gun.

The dog went off with the speed of a cougar, grabbed the mime's arm and tried to wrestle him down. The fugitive struggled and hit back wildly, lashing out with a lethal-looking knife. Then went on running with the dog still snapping at his heels.

'STOP!' ordered Brewster one final time, then raised his pistol and took aim.

52

For them, of course, it meant the end. There could be no future together. What she'd missed out was the most significant part. Though the verdict was bound to be misadventure, Brewster's action had irrevocably damaged what he'd been hoping to salvage from what they had had. He knew that for sure, from the look on her face when they had broken the news.

He stood outside the coroner's court, leaning against his car. Not the official one today; he had come as a private individual to offer sympathy and pay his respects to the dead. A smattering of newsmen were gathered outside to hear the final verdict. The sky was murky; it looked like rain and matched the feeling in his heart.

With a swish of tyres, a Rolls-Royce pulled up and parked discreetly fifty yards away. Dr Rousseau nodded to Brewster but kept his distance. At least it meant she would not be alone; he wished the pair of them well. He was glad to know she'd no longer have to struggle.

If anyone were to carry the blame, it was Esmée Morell for contracting German measles which had left her unborn foetus permanently damaged. A perfect baby in every other way, his slow responses had become apparent only as he approached the age when normally he would start talking. Since his parents were wholly preoccupied by the pursuit of their starry careers, it had fallen solely upon his sister to help him learn to communicate. Nobody else had noticed or even cared. When the deafness was medically diagnosed and it was clear that he would never become an actor, his parents had turned their backs on him.

Celeste was the one who had taught him to sign and later also to lip-read. With proper care he might have lived a far more useful life. Instead he grew up a social outcast, held back from normal development because of his mother's distaste. All Esmée cared about was perfection. First, through jealousy, she had ruined her daughter, then, later, destroyed her son.

An usher appeared on the courthouse steps. The morning session had ended. He carried a statement to read to the press, declaring the verdict as misadventure, just as Brewster had predicted. They pressed round him to shake his hand but could do nothing to ease the ache in his heart. He had sacrificed his emotional future by doing his duty as a policeman.

Celeste appeared, on her lawyer's arm, and the doctor stepped forward to greet her. Grief had added immeasurably to her beauty. She stood in silence in her plain black suit while the lawyer made a brief public statement, then followed him down the steps to the waiting car. When she reached the spot where

Brewster was standing, she walked straight by as if he were not even there. He stood and watched as they drove away. She never even turned her head.

Of course there had been an official inquiry but his service record remained unblemished. Oberon Forrester had been killed while resisting arrest. Since Brewster had now been passed as fit, he'd asked permission to return to Baghdad where he felt his firearms skills would be better employed.

There were things, however, to clear up first, not the least of which was one final walk with his partner. He would miss the playground and his dreams of having children, but the biggest hurt would be saying goodbye to Burgess.

<u>HIDDEN AGENDA</u>

Carol Smith

Devastated by the shocking news that an old schoolfriend, Suzy Palmer, faces execution in Louisiana for the murder of her children, London rabbi, Deborah Hirsch, enlists the aid of her former classmates in an attempt to get her off. The Suzy they've known and loved all these years could never hurt a fly; she can't be anything but innocent.

As Death Row draws steadily closer, the friends slowly piece together what has happened. Aided by Miss Holbrook, Suzy's feisty former art teacher, and Markus, a jazz musician who's following the case in New Orleans, they recall their thirty-year friendship – and realise that even more shocking than Suzy's plight is the knowledge that one of their number has betrayed her.

VANISHING POINT

Carol Smith

When Frankie, mid-forties, sees the unforgettable face of her long-lost love in a passing train, she turns straight round and goes after him. For she, more than anyone, knows he is dead; was there when it happen, attended the inquest and later served time for his manslaughter.

Frankie, Cristina, Cassandra, Jenny and Pippa . . . five women living quite separate lives except for one crucial fact. Cristina, the spoilt Brazilian ex-model; Cassie, the dignified lady of class; Jenny, who runs a fashionable eatery while raising a child on her own; and Pippa, the much younger mistress, now pregnant with his twins. Each of them has devoted her life to the same duplicitous man.

Antwerp, Paris, Venice, Rio, Bath . . . their lives are very widespread. But when the circles begin to intersect, the only possible ending is murder.

Other bestselling titles available by mail: